Praise f

"... a perfect comi[...]
a bree[...]

"Like Beverly Cleary's beloved and headstrong heroine, Ramona [...]y,
Zibby Payne is not afraid to take a stand. Her message to girls is a fine one ..."
– Robin Abcarian, Senior Features Correspondent, *LA Times*

"... readers won't be able to put it down and parents everywhere
will approve." – *Mom Central*

"The issues of friends and enemies are timeless, and even readers new
to the 'Zibby Payne' series will slip smoothly into the candid, funny,
nonpreachy account of how a tough kid betrays the best in herself and
then battles to put things right." – *Booklist*

"... funny and engaging sixth-grade characters ..." – *School Library Journal*

"It's hard not to like Zibby Payne. She's a plucky girl and a talented athlete
who does her own thing on her own terms ... fresh and endearing with her
confidence, savvy, and sense of humour ... Zibby Payne's adventures have the
humour and momentum to become a well-loved series."
– *Montreal Review of Books*

"... reminiscent of Beverly Cleary's Ramona, as she is a strong-minded
character with a flair for the dramatic ... a humorous tone that is perfect for
engaging young readers." – *Children's Literature*

"Bell has created a girl who's not afraid to be herself. A rare treat."
– Mary Hogan, author of *Susanna Sees Stars*

Featured on The TODAY Show and in FamilyFun!

Now Available:

ZIBBY PAYNE & THE TRIO TROUBLE
978-1-897073-78-0

ZIBBY PAYNE & THE PARTY PROBLEM
978-1-897073-69-8

ZIBBY PAYNE & THE DRAMA TRAUMA
978-1-897073-47-6

ZIBBY PAYNE & THE WONDERFUL, TERRIBLE TOMBOY EXPERIMENT
978-1-897073-39-1

ZIBBY PAYNE

PAYNE

& THE RED CARPET REVOLT

Zibby Payne & the Red Carpet Revolt
Text © 2008 Alison Bell

Published by Lobster Press™
1620 Sherbrooke Street West, Suites C & D
Montréal, Québec   H3H 1C9
Tel. (514) 904-1100 • Fax (514) 904-1101 • www.lobsterpress.com

Publisher: Alison Fripp
Editor: Meghan Nolan
Editorial Assistant: Brynn Smith-Raska
Graphic Design & Production: Tammy Desnoyers

Library and Archives Canada Cataloguing in Publication

Bell, Alison
       Zibby Payne & the red carpet revolt / Alison Bell.

(Zibby Payne series)
ISBN 978-1-897073-98-8

       I. Title. II. Title: Zibby Payne and the red carpet revolt.
III. Series: Bell, Alison. Zibby Payne series.

PZ7.B41528Zir 2008   j813'.6   C2008-901764-1

The Academy Awards is a trademark of the Academy of Motion Pictures Arts and
Sciences; **Adidas** is a trademark of adidas America, Inc.; **Barbie** is a trademark of
Mattel, Inc.; **The Beatles** is a trademark of Apple Corps Limited Corporation;
Blistex is a trademark of Blistex Bracken Limited; **Cruella de Vil** is a trademark of
Disney Enterprises, Inc.; **eBay** is a trademark of eBay Inc.; **The Eagles** is a trademark
of Eagles, Ltd.; **Girl Scout** is a trademark of Girl Scouts of the United States of
America Corporation; **iPod** is a trademark of Apple Inc. Corporation; **Kleenex** is a
trademark of Kimberly Clark; **Mickey Mouse** is a trademark of Disney Enterprises,
Inc.; **Powerpoint** is a trademark of Microsoft Corporation.

Printed and bound in Canada.

Text is printed on Rolland Enviro 100 Book,
100% recycled post-consumer fibre.

To the boys: Jim, Cole, and Hank.

– Alison Bell

ZIBBY PAYNE

& THE RED CARPET REVOLT

written by

Alison Bell

Lobster Press ™

CHAPTER 1

NO LAUGHING MATTER

"Yippee! No more school today," Zibby Payne whispered to her best friend Sarah as they trooped into the school auditorium.

"We can just sit back and relax," said Sarah with a smile.

The two girls were spending the last hour of the day attending a sixth-grade assembly. Their teacher, Miss Cannon, hadn't told them what the assembly was about, but Zibby knew any assembly had to be better than filling out another grammar worksheet or correcting the latest social studies quiz.

Plus, it was Friday, and this was the perfect way to kick off the weekend. Zibby was already mentally preparing for the fun things she was going to do Saturday and Sunday, such as play soccer and walk to the local ice cream shop, The Scoop, with Sarah and her other best friend Gertrude.

Sarah and Zibby sat down next to each other in the auditorium. Amber, their "sometimes-friend" who lately had turned into "no friend at all," sat down in front of them with her two wannabe pals, Camille and Savannah. As soon as she'd settled into her seat, Amber turned around to face Zibby.

"So whatcha doing this weekend?" she asked.

"Hanging out," Zibby replied. She didn't bother to mention soccer since she knew Amber would disapprove. Amber not only hated soccer, she ranked any sweat-related activity at the top of her *not* to-do list.

"What are *you* doing?" Zibby asked politely.

"It's a TBF all the way," smiled Amber.

"Huh?" asked Zibby.

"TBF – Total Beauty Fest," replied Amber impatiently. She then looked at Sarah. "*You* knew what that stood for, right?"

"No," said Sarah, shrugging her shoulders.

Amber shook her head as if Zibby and Sarah were both totally hopeless, then continued. "Anyway, I'm getting a mani-pedi and a haircut. And my mom even said I could get this special orange-peel facial that all the celebs are getting. I'm so excited!"

"Sounds like fun," Zibby said to Amber. But as soon as Amber turned back around in her chair, Zibby whispered "Not!" under her breath to Sarah. She couldn't think of anything worse than sitting around having orange peels – which belong in the trash – rubbed on her face.

Zibby would have commented to Sarah more about how dumb Amber's Big Beauty Weekend sounded, but Miss Cannon stood in front of them and clapped her hands together.

"Settle down everyone, please," she said in her Serious Teacher Voice. "First of all, I want to make an announcement. We've chosen a date for the sixth-grade dance. It will be on Saturday night the twentieth, so mark your calendars."

Zibby felt a stab of excitement. The dance was four weeks away, and she couldn't wait! It was the most important day of the year for the sixth graders besides graduation. At the dance, held in the school cafeteria, they ate pizza and drank soft drinks, and the school even brought in a jukebox each year. They got to hang out with their friends, listen to music, and stay up until 10:00 pm!

"We'll be choosing a theme for the dance soon, so get your thinking caps on," continued Miss Cannon.

Zibby was excited about that too. Each year the students voted on a theme for the dance, and Zibby had a really good idea she thought could win.

"And now," Miss Cannon continued, "I'd like you to focus your attention on our librarian, Miss Wendt, who will explain the new library coding system."

In front of Zibby, Amber groaned and whispered loudly, "Oh no – this is gonna be a total snooze-o-rama."

"Shhh," whispered Zibby. While a lecture on coding library books *did* sound a little dull, she really liked Miss Wendt, who often let her take out four books at once when three was the official limit. Zibby wouldn't stand for Amber saying anything mean about the librarian or her lecture.

Miss Wendt, a short woman with black hair, stood up from the center of the room. Next to her was a small table on which was a laptop computer.

"Hello, readers. I've put together an exciting Power-point presentation, so get ready to explore the mysteries of library science!"

Miss Cannon dimmed the lights, and a picture of a book flashed on the screen in the front of the room.

"Take a close look at this book spine, which contains a combination of the letters and numbers F102x," Miss Wendt said energetically. "You might be asking, what do all those letters and numbers mean? Well, let me tell you!"

Zibby blinked her eyes open and shut as Miss Wendt went on and on about "subcategories," "classifications," and "subclassifications." While she hated to admit it, Amber was right. This assembly was a snore. A big one.

In front of her, Amber started to squirm in her seat, and then she whispered something to Camille.

The two girls giggled. Savannah looked over, and seeing her two friends laughing, she began to giggle as well.

How rude, thought Zibby.

But a few moments later, she was feeling pretty rude herself because she was barely able to keep her eyes open. How nice would it really be if she fell asleep right in the middle of Miss Wendt's talk? There had to be a way to wake up. Then she had an idea. She reached into the pocket of her jeans and pulled out a piece of sugarless bubble gum she'd been carrying around for a few days. Chewing gum was against the school rules, but this was an emergency. She popped the piece of gum in her mouth and began chewing ferociously. Her tactic worked: The more she chewed, the more alert she felt.

For the rest of the assembly, Amber & Company continued to giggle and squirm. Twice Miss Cannon had to tell them to settle down. After the assembly, as the kids lined up to return to class and grab their backpacks and go home, Miss Cannon reprimanded the three girls.

"Amber, Camille, and Savannah, I'm extremely disappointed in you," she said sternly in front of the entire class. "Everyone else managed to pay attention during Miss Wendt's talk except for you. I'm sorry to say there will be consequences for this." She pulled on her pinky finger, which she did whenever she got nervous or upset. "All three of you will attend Saturday school tomorrow. Please report to the principal's office at 9:00 am. Your parents can pick you up at 4:00 pm."

"No way!" Amber gasped, flipping back her hair in shock. "I'm busy tomorrow – super busy with super-important stuff!"

"Me, too," said Camille.

"Me, three," echoed Savannah.

"You should have thought of that before you displayed such dreadful manners to Miss Wendt," said Miss Cannon firmly.

The three girls looked at Miss Cannon with shocked expressions on their faces.

"Miss Cannon, I do not *do* Saturday school," Amber said.

"I don't usually either," answered Miss Cannon. "I don't want to spend my Saturday sitting with you while I could be going to my yoga class. But there must be consequences."

"But you don't understand – I really can't miss what I've got planned!" persisted Amber.

"Well then," Miss Cannon considered, "I could think of another punishment. You could all miss the sixth-grade dance, for example."

"Miss the sixth-grade dance? No way!" wailed Amber.

"Okay, then. I'll see you at 9:00 am tomorrow. End of discussion." Miss Cannon began leading the class walking toward the classroom.

Zibby couldn't help but smile. *That's what Amber gets for planning her entire weekend around orange peels*, she thought to herself.

But then, Amber cried out, "Miss Cannon, wait! I've got a better suggestion. You were just talking about manners, and actually I know tons about them. My aunt used to be a beauty queen, and she's taught me a lot about being respectful and polite. Maybe I did laugh during the assembly – and I *am* totally sorry about that. But I can make it up to you by teaching a manners class for the three of us ... and anyone else you think may need it."

Zibby couldn't help but snicker. Amber? Bragging about being respectful? Ha! Everyone knew she was the reigning Queen of Mean at Lincoln Elementary and the only thing she respected was her high opinion of herself.

"Good try, Amber, but it's a no-go," said Miss Cannon.

"Come on, I really *do* know a lot about manners," insisted Amber.

"Hmm," said Miss Cannon skeptically.

"It's true!"

Miss Cannon looked hard at Amber. "You really think you can do this?"

"For sure, yes."

"And what do you think about this, girls?" Miss Cannon asked Camille and Savannah.

"We're good with it," answered Camille.

Miss Cannon hesitated. "Well, I guess that way I wouldn't have to miss my yoga class. But when and where would you teach this class?"

Amber thought for a moment. "At lunch. I'd be happy to give up my lunches for a good cause like this."

Miss Cannon pulled on her pinky one more time, and then nodded her head. "Since the sixth-grade dance *is* coming up, and last year the students got a bit rowdy, it's not a bad time to be brushing up on manners. After all, we want our dance to be a success. So you're on, Amber. You give up your lunches for the next two weeks to teach your crowd some manners and I'll forget Saturday School tomorrow. You can start on Monday."

"Thanks, Miss Cannon," Amber flashed her a big smile. She then linked arms with her two sidekicks, and the three headed off to class.

Camille and Savannah didn't look upset at all, but Zibby couldn't help feeling sorry for them and their lunchtime fate. "What a nightmare – stuck in manner's school – with Amber as the teacher! Thank goodness it's not me!" she said to herself as she absentmindedly blew a small bubble with the piece of gum in her mouth. The bubble burst, making a sharp crackling sound.

"Zibby!" Miss Cannon turned to glare at her. "You know there is no gum chewing allowed in school, and especially no bubble blowing! It looks like *your* manners could use a refresher course as well. So you'll be joining Amber's manners club too."

"What?" Zibby's mouth dropped open so far that her gum fell out and dropped to the floor.

Her? In Amber's manners class?

No way!

CHAPTER 2

MANNERS BY MOI

"I'm doomed!" Zibby complained as she walked home from school that day with Sarah and Gertrude. "Just when I was feeling so happy about the weekend and the dance, now I have to go to manners school!"

"My mom has some ear plugs she takes on airplane rides with her – maybe you can use them," offered Gertrude as she adjusted her vintage crocheted poncho. "Maybe you can just stick them in and nod a lot, and Amber will never know you're not hearing a word she's saying."

"Yeah, but knowing Amber, she'd notice, and then she'd tell on me and I'd get in even more trouble," said Zibby.

"Maybe it won't be as bad as you think," Sarah said, placing her hand reassuringly on Zibby's shoulder. "Plus, it's only for a few weeks."

"That will feel like a few years!" said Zibby. "And this means I have to give up my lunchtime soccer."

Most every day at lunch, Zibby pulled on her Adidas cleats and played soccer with the boys. She'd worked hard to be one of the best players out on the field, and she resented having soccer taken away from her – especially for manners lessons … with Amber!

"I think it might be kind of fun," said Sarah quietly.

"Fun?" yelled Zibby. She stopped walking and turned to

stare at Sarah, sure that Sarah had gone temporarily crazy.

"Yes, fun," Sarah continued smoothly, not paying any attention to Zibby's raised voice because she was used to Zibby's dramatic flare-ups. "You know how in all those old movies, everyone looks so glamorous and says 'dear' and 'darling' all the time and the women wear dresses and gloves even if they're just sitting around the house? Like in *The Philadelphia Story* with Katharine Hepburn and Cary Grant. I love that movie – it's so romantic."

"Well I've never seen it! And I don't want to act like I'm in some old movie or be like Katharine Heartburn or whatever her name is," said Zibby, frowning.

"I doubt Amber's seen any old movies anyway," said Gertrude. "The only things she probably ever watches are shows about celebrities or makeovers."

"What does Amber know about manners anyway?" Zibby snapped one of her backpack straps in frustration. "She thinks it's being polite when she calls someone a 'loser' rather than a 'total loser'!"

"Maybe she'll teach 'mean manners,'" said Gertrude, laughing. "You know, the best way to insult someone, or how to make a snotty post on someone's wall, stuff like that." Gertrude smiled at her own joke.

"*You* can smile, because *you* don't have to go!" said Zibby.

"You know what? I'll do the classes with you," announced Sarah.

"You will?" Zibby's eyes opened wide in surprise – and joy.

"Like I said, it might be fun and I'm curious to see what Amber is going to teach. Plus, this way I at least get to spend lunch with you, Zibby." Sarah, a self-admitted "klutz," didn't play soccer and missed not hanging out with Zibby at lunchtime.

"Do you want to come too?" Zibby looked at Gertrude.

"No thanks," said Gertrude, shaking her head. "I'm too busy – cleaning my paintbrushes." Gertrude, an artist, was always painting watercolor pictures in the sketchbook she carried around, and she did clean her paintbrushes a lot. But Zibby knew this wasn't about paintbrushes.

"Some excuse!" said Zibby.

"Can I help it if I don't want to be around Amber any more than I have to?" asked Gertrude. She'd only moved to Lincoln Elementary a few months ago but had already had a few run-ins with The Sixth-Grade Diva.

"No," said Zibby, not blaming her friend one bit.

"I'll be with you, Zibby, so it will be all right," said Sarah.

For the first time since learning she was in manners school, Zibby smiled. With Sarah by her side, how bad could Amber's class really be?

* * *

Monday morning when the lunch bell rang, Zibby and Sarah walked over to the tables in the cafeteria. Well, actually Sarah had to drag Zibby, but eventually the two made it. Amber, along with Camille and Savannah, was sitting at Table 12, where she and her "peeps" sat every day. She had a wooden picnic basket by her side.

"Now that you're here, we can begin." Amber motioned for the girls to sit down and then she opened the lid of the picnic basket.

"Welcome to Manners 101 – Amber-style," she smiled. "For our first lesson, taught by *moi* – and *moi* alone – I'm going to teach you how to properly set a table! Ta-da," she reached into the picnic basket and pulled out a stack of plates, some water glasses, pink cloth napkins, and a pile of silverware.

"How to properly set a table?" Zibby asked in disbelief. "What does any of this have to do with being polite and respectful?"

"Nothing," replied Amber as she began to arrange the plates and silverware on the table.

"But isn't that what you told Miss Cannon you were going to teach?" persisted Zibby.

"No," said Amber briskly, setting a soup spoon beside a plate. "All I said was that I was going to teach manners. I never said exactly *what* I was going to teach. And I *am* talking about a *type* of manners – table manners."

"But why do we want to learn about that? That's for little old ladies who go to country clubs," said Zibby.

"Zibby, Zibby, Zibby," Amber sighed. "Do you ever watch that TV show *Rich, Blonde & Bored*?

"No ... what the heck is that?" asked Zibby. She mainly only watched sports and movies.

"That new show about all those rich girls in New York City who go to parties and dance with these really cute guys from England who are lords or dukes," Camille piped up.

"Uh, no. I haven't seen it," said Zibby.

"How about *My Very Special Day*, where girls have elaborate birthday parties thrown for them?" asked Amber.

"No," said Zibby.

Amber sighed. "Ever watch the Academy Awards?"

"Of course," answered Zibby testily.

"Do you ever hear about all those post-parties the stars go to?"

"I've heard *you* talk about them," said Zibby.

"Well, then let me explain how important table manners are this way: If you're ever at one of those fancy post-parties with white tablecloths and waiters in tuxedos, you'll want to know which fork to eat your salad with. I mean, come on, you don't want to look like a loser or anything, especially in front of all those stars and paparazzi!"

"But I'm never going to a post-Academy Awards party," said Zibby.

"Dream, Zibby, you've got to dream," Amber said sharply. "I plan on going to tons of them, and when I do, I'm going to know the difference between my dinner fork and my fish fork."

For emphasis, she picked up a fork and waved it in front of Zibby's face.

"Forget the forks. I'm outta here," said Zibby as she turned around, getting ready to bolt.

"Wait, Zibby," said Sarah, clearing her throat as a warning. "Here comes Miss Cannon."

She looked up as Miss Cannon walked in their direction. *Shoot.* Now she had to stay.

But then she had an idea that cheered her up. When Miss Cannon saw the ridiculous lessons Amber was teaching, she was going to be mad. She'd disband the class and stick Amber back in Saturday School where she belonged.

"How is the manners class going?" Miss Cannon asked,

descending on them with a smile. "Oh Sarah, you're here too," she added, looking surprised to see her.

"I thought I'd check it out," nodded Sarah.

"It's going awesome," interrupted Amber. "I realized, Miss Cannon, that to really learn how to be respectful, we had to start with the basics, like table manners, then move on from there. So I've brought five table settings from my mother's best china and silverware collection, and I'm showing the girls what to do if they ever eat at a fine restaurant or go to a dinner party."

Zibby turned expectantly to Miss Cannon, eagerly awaiting what she knew was going to be her disapproving reply about Amber's off-target subject material.

But Miss Cannon smiled and nodded as if Amber had discovered the True Meaning of Being Polite & Respectful.

"Good idea, Amber. I've noticed that kids today sometimes eat like animals. This is so needed. Thank you."

"You're welcome," said Amber, the dimple in her cheek deepening as she gave a smug smile.

"But Miss Cannon, knowing which fork to use has nothing to do with being polite! This is totally a waste of time!" Zibby yelled.

Miss Cannon raised her eyebrows. "I don't want to be unkind, Zibby, but I've seen how you attack your sandwiches at lunch, and I *don't* think this is a waste of time for you."

Zibby looked sheepishly down at the ground. Miss Cannon *did* have a point. But was it her fault that by lunchtime she was starving, and her favorite sandwich – salmon and pickles – was a little messy to eat?

"Carry on, girls," said Miss Cannon.

"We will, Miss Cannon," said Amber. She finished setting five places and then began blabbing on about the proper use of a dinner fork versus a salad fork and when to use a fish fork.

Help! Zibby said to herself. She was so sure she was going to get out of Amber's class, but here she was, still sitting there. She was going to have to come up with a way to survive anyway – and quick – because she didn't think she could last much longer if she didn't!

CHAPTER 3

TAKING A STAB AT IT

"I know what will make this class fun," Zibby said to herself as Amber picked up a soup spoon and began lecturing about how soup must always be sipped, never slurped.

Her older brother, Anthony, had taught her a really cool trick that would come in handy right now. She grabbed a soup spoon off the table and blew some hot air on the hollowed-out part to make it sticky. Then she hung the spoon on the tip of her nose and let go. The spoon stayed, perfectly balanced!

"Cool, huh?" she said proudly to the group.

"Come on, Zibby, quit messing around," said Amber crossly.

"Gross! You're getting icky nose germs on the spoon!" said Camille.

Zibby blinked and the spoon came clattering off her nose. She smiled sheepishly, but no one smiled back except for Sarah.

"So-rry!" Zibby said, putting the spoon back on the table. She slumped into her chair and checked her watch. There were still eighteen minutes left of lunch. This was going to be the longest lunch *ever*. And what about eating? She was so hungry, her stomach was rumbling.

"Do we *ever* get to eat lunch?" she asked.

"I'm almost done with my lesson, and when I am, we

23

can all test out our new manners using the place settings," said Amber.

Finally, after what seemed like forever to Zibby but was only about five minutes, Amber wrapped up her talk and they were free to begin eating.

Zibby placed her salmon and pickle sandwich on her plate, along with some chips and gummy worms. She was reaching for a gummy worm when Amber yelled, "Not with your fingers – use a fork!"

"But gummy worms are finger foods," protested Zibby.

"When you're out with at a dinner party, with, like, let's say, mega-cutie Fabrio Fabricio, do you think he wants to see you eat with your grubby little fingers?" asked Amber.

Zibby rolled her eyes. Who cares, since she didn't plan on going to a dinner party any time soon, especially not with Fabrio Fabricio, who was the lead singer of this barfy boy band called BB5 that Amber was infatuated with. But to get Amber off her case, she grabbed the first fork she could find – the fish fork – and stabbed a purple and orange gummy worm with it. But it missed, and the worm shimmied off the plate and onto the table.

Zibby raised the fork again and slammed it down on the worm hard. The fork missed yet again, and this time it got stuck in the wooden table. When Zibby pulled the fork out, the prongs bent backward.

"Uh oh," Zibby was saying to herself just as Amber screamed, "Zibby Payne, what have you done to my mother's fork?"

"I was using it, just like you told me to!" answered Zibby. "I didn't mean to hurt it," she stared at the broken utensil in dismay.

"Let me have it," Amber commanded. She grabbed the fork from Zibby's hand and fiddled with the prongs, but they wouldn't go back all the way.

"My mom is gonna be so mad," Amber said. "This fish fork has been in my family for *three* generations. It's really special." She glared at Zibby.

"I'm sorry," said Zibby. "Here, give it to me. I'm sure my dad can fix it. He's good at fixing things. Really good." Zibby thought Amber was overreacting, but still, she felt guilty for what she'd done and she wanted to make it right.

"Okay, but please, be gentle with it," Amber handed the fork back to Zibby.

"I will, I promise," said Zibby, shoving it as delicately as she could into her jean skirt pocket for safekeeping.

Amber then swooped up all of Zibby's silverware and put it back into the basket.

"I've changed my mind," said Amber. "Go ahead and use your fingers – for the worms, for everything."

"Great," said Zibby, picking up a worm and throwing it into her mouth, just happy that the first class was over.

* * *

"One down, a zillion to go," Zibby said to Sarah on the walk home later that day.

"It wasn't *that* bad," admitted Sarah. "I always wondered which fork to use first."

"Sarah!" Zibby interrupted her. "How can you say it wasn't 'that bad'? It was horrible! Horrible squared!"

Sarah shrugged. "I can't help it. I told you I kind of like learning about old-fashioned rules."

"Well, I don't," yelled Zibby. "I live by my own rules! Be yourself, have fun, and don't ever worry about which fork to use."

"And that's why I love you, Zibby," Sarah smiled. "Even if I *do* care about forks – a little, at least."

"Oh well, whatever Amber's problem is, I'm just glad the first lesson is over. Because anything she teaches from now on has to better than that!"

But as soon as Zibby got to lunch the next day for Manners Lesson Number Two, she realized she'd spoken too quickly. Amber had written up an agenda outlining the rest of the week's lessons. When Zibby looked at it, she almost fell over:

Tuesday: Elbows off the Table: More table manners by moi!

Wednesday: Text Messaging Manners: How to text-message one BFF while you're talking to another without either BFF knowing!

Thursday: Accessory Essentials: When to wear faux pearls versus when to wear the real deal!

Friday: Beauty Manners: Get gorgeous now, in style!

Zibby threw down the paper in disgust.
Oh no, she thought.
These are even *worse* than the first lesson.
Way worse!

CHAPTER 4

A LUCKY BREAK

"Wake me up when it's over," Zibby whispered to Sarah after a long, grueling week of manners lessons. Now it was Friday, and she was totally zoning out as Amber went over her "beauty manners basics."

"And so, don't forget," Amber droned on, "when you go to your hairstylist, always leave at least a 20 percent tip. For example, if your haircut cost $40, you'd leave an $8 tip."

The last part, however, got Zibby's attention. "Forty dollars?" Zibby sputtered. "My haircuts cost $14 at *Quick Cut.* And that's *with* the tip."

"My mom cuts my hair," said Sarah.

"I feel so sorry for you two," said Amber, looking at them as if they were the two Most Pathetic Girls on the Planet.

"I used to go to *Quick Cut* when I was a kid, but now my mom takes me to her stylist, Jean Pierre, who works at *Le Studio,*" said Camille.

"That's funny. I thought you *still were* a kid," quipped Zibby.

"Come on now, I'm eleven," said Camille. "Sixth graders aren't kids anymore." She looked at Zibby and at her sporty T-shirt and her hair pulled back casually into a ponytail. "Well, most of us aren't anyway," she added.

"I'm glad I'm a kid if it means not going to snooty salons

and shelling out big bucks to have some guy with a name I can't even pronounce trim my ponytail," yelled Zibby, which pretty much ended the conversation ... and the lesson for the day.

"Okay peeps, see you back here next week," Amber said as she quickly packed up her things.

How am I ever gonna stand another week of this? Zibby was thinking to herself when Miss Cannon approached.

"Hello, girls," she said. "I'm sorry I haven't been able to drop by lately – I've been really busy with paperwork. But it seems like you've all been working hard. So how's it been going?"

Zibby started to say "Terrible," then bit her tongue.

"Terrific," Sarah covered for Zibby. "She said, 'Terrific'."

"Good," said Miss Cannon. "And now, girls," she said as she looked at Amber, Camille, and Savannah, "I trust there will be no more giggling during assemblies?"

"Right," the three girls said in unison.

"And no more gum chewing or bubble blowing?" She looked at Zibby.

"Never again," said Zibby, wondering where Miss Cannon's questions were leading.

"Then I think that you have all learned your 'lesson,' excuse the pun, and your manners classes are finished. You can get back to your normal lunch periods next week. Good work again, and I look forward to seeing your manners in action."

Zibby couldn't believe her good luck at getting out of the lessons a week early. "Thank you, thank you, thank you, Miss Cannon," she said, jumping up and down.

"I see you've gotten the 'thank you' part of manners down, Zibby," Miss Cannon said.

"Yes, I have," said Zibby, trying not to choke on her words since Amber had never even covered such manners basics as "thank you" and "please."

After Miss Cannon walked away, Amber gave a big sigh.

"I'm so bummed. I already had next week all planned out! I was going to teach you all how to curtsy. I saw on *Rich, Blonde & Bored* that curtsying is coming back in at all those prep school dinner parties on the Upper East Side of Manhattan. Waltzing's in too, and my aunt said she could teach us."

"And thank you again!" Zibby yelled to Miss Cannon's back, even more relieved than before to be done with Amber's class.

But Camille and Savannah's faces fell disappointedly at the news of what they would be missing.

Zibby ignored them and focused on making her escape. "It's been a real blast, but now it's time for me to blast off," she said. "Come on, Sarah, let's go."

The two girls were about to leave when Amber yelled, "Hey wait a minute! Don't anyone move. I've got a great idea! We can still have our classes, even if Miss Cannon isn't making us. We'll just keep doing it on our own. And we'll invite even more girls. Same time. Same place. Won't that be fun?"

"No, actually I *don't* think it will be fun," said Zibby. "You all just go ahead and knock yourselves out curtsying and waltzing, but I won't be doing it, because I don't have to."

"You won't?" asked Amber with a look of disbelief that said anyone who didn't want to learn to curtsy was a total twit. "Your loss then."

"Yes it is," said Zibby, pulling Sarah away with her. "But we'll just have to live with it."

"And Zibby, don't forget about the fish fork. My mom wants it back – pronto!" added Amber.

Woops. Zibby felt a pang of guilt. She'd forgotten about it. "I will – I promise," she said. And then, still holding onto Sarah's arm, she hurried away from the table to class.

"Am I ever glad that class is over," she muttered to Sarah.

"The table manners stuff was interesting, and some of the beauty manners, but the rest is dumb," said Sarah.

Zibby swung open the door to the classroom. "All I can say is, please never mention manners to me again. I just want to forget that the whole week ever happened!"

* * *

Forgetting about Amber's manners lessons wasn't as easy as Zibby had hoped, however.

On Monday, before school, Amber announced to all the sixth-grade girls that she would be continuing her classes at lunch, beginning with a curtsying lesson. That day at lunch, Camille, Savannah, and a few other of Amber's closest "peeps" showed up. The next day, four more girls. And by Wednesday, there were over a dozen girls huddled over at Table 12, including some of Zibby's friends – Lyla, Katherine, Grace, Franny, and Vanessa.

"I can't believe they're all taking her class now too!" Zibby said to Sarah and Gertrude as they sat down to eat their lunches. "Look at them all! I wonder what stupid, snotty thing they're learning today." She watched as Amber pulled out what looked like a tube of mascara and some lip gloss from her backpack.

"Yuck! Must be more makeup manners," said Zibby.

"Hmm," Sarah said as she strained to get a better look. "I wonder what type of makeup they're using. I can't really see, but it looks like La Di Da cosmetics. My mom uses those – they're really good."

"Please, Sarah, can we talk about something else?" asked Zibby. "Something interesting, for a change. Like the sixth-grade dance!"

"So tell me more about it," said Gertrude. "What's it supposed to be like?"

"It's the best," said Zibby. "I heard all about it from last year's sixth graders. They play really cool music on this jukebox – last year they played a lot of classic rock like our favorites, the Beatles and the Eagles. And everyone dances ... well, I don't plan to, but a lot do! And the teachers always get this special pizza from Pizza Planet. It's called 'The Everything' and they make it special for Lincoln Elementary."

"It's got everything on it you can think of – even chocolate chips!" said Sarah.

"Sounds ... pretty gross," said Gertrude.

"No, it's really good," said Zibby. "Plus, it's tradition. They've been doing it for like seven years."

"So what do you wear?" asked Gertrude.

"Whatever you want! There's no dress code or anything," said Zibby. "I'll probably wear my usual – comfortable clothes and my high-tops."

"My mom already bought me a new dress to wear," said Sarah. Unlike Zibby, she was a total dresses girl and wore either a dress or a skirt most every day.

"Maybe I'll wear my new palazzo pants I got at *Déjà You*," said Gertrude, who shopped mainly at used-clothing stores.

"Hey, and since we're talking about the dance, want to hear the theme I'm going to suggest?" asked Zibby.

"Sure," chirped her friends.

"*Kick Up Your Heels*. Get it? It relates to the dancing, but also to my favorite thing ... kicking a soccer ball. I thought I could maybe bring in my portable soccer net and set it up by the jukebox, and every time you select a song, you take a shot!"

"Nice," smiled Sarah.

"And such a surprise that you'd pick a soccer theme," teased Gertrude.

"I hope it wins," said Zibby, wondering what her competition would be, when suddenly her attention was diverted by the sound of high-pitched screams coming from Table 12.

CHAPTER 5

AMBER'S BIG IDEA

"Are you guys okay?" Zibby asked as the three girls ran over to Table 12 to see what was going on.

"We're fine," replied Katherine. "We're all just so excited about the news that we had to scream!"

"What news?" asked Zibby.

"Yeah, what's up?" asked Gertrude.

"I've got some big news about *moi* and about all my peeps!" screeched Amber. "I've been talking to my parents about the classes I've been teaching, and they've decided to throw us a ball to show off our manners!"

"A what?" asked Zibby, wondering if she'd heard correctly.

"A ball," repeated Amber, sounding annoyed.

"Like Cinderella?" Zibby asked, holding back a snort of laughter.

"No, not like Cinderella," Amber frowned. "Like a debutante ball – you know, where girls get introduced to high society. That's what I'm talking about!"

She whipped out a glossy magazine from her backpack, flipped to a page, and thrust it at Zibby. On the page was a picture of girls dressed up in evening gowns and boys in dark suits. "See? This ball was held just last month in Manhattan. This girl here," she slapped the page on the face of a blonde girl, "looked for her dress for six months and had three fittings to make sure it fit perfectly. But my ball's going to be even better. We're going to walk down a red carpet just like at the Academy Awards!"

"A red carpet?" Zibby gasped. What world was Amber living in? No sixth grader threw a ball with a red carpet.

"My aunt found one on eBay. A real one. And she's getting it for me. Oh, and plus, we're all going to go to the ball in a limo. My dad has a friend who's a limo driver!"

"Seriously? This is ridiculous," Zibby whispered to Gertrude and Sarah, who nodded in agreement.

But the rest of the girls didn't think it was a crazy idea at all.

"Limos are sooo cool," gushed Grace. "My sister rode in one once. She got to stick her head out of the sunroof and scream."

"I always wanted to walk down a red carpet!" piped up Camille.

"Do you think I could have a dress fitting?" asked Katherine eagerly.

"And we're gonna have a chocolate fountain!" squealed Savannah.

"What's that?" asked Sarah.

"Yeah," said Zibby.

Amber sighed. "Duh! What do you think? It's a fountain that chocolate comes out of and you dip fruit and cookies into it. Don't you guys know anything?"

"No, not about debutante balls, thank goodness," said Zibby.

But Amber didn't seem to hear. She just kept rambling on.

"And we're all going to have our hair done and get manis and pedis so we all look just as fantabulous as these girls in the magazines!" She waved the magazine around again.

"Oh, and peeps, in order to prepare for the ball, we're going to really have to step up our manners lessons. You're all going to have to get ready for your big debutante debut."

"Oh no, she's talking about her lessons again," Zibby whispered to her two close friends. "Let's leave." The three backed away from the crowd.

"This is the dumbest thing I've heard of in my whole life," Zibby sputtered once they were out of Amber's earshot. "I thought manners class was bad enough, but a manners *ball*? If I have to spend the next few weeks listening to everyone go on and on about it, I'm going to go nuts!"

"Don't even worry about it," Gertrude cut in. "This ball of hers is never going to happen. It's just some fantasy Amber's created."

"Yeah, she's just trying to be the center of attention – as always," said Sarah.

"I hope so," sighed Zibby. "And even if she somehow does throw this ball of hers, at least I don't have to be part of it."

The bell rang, signaling lunch was over. Zibby was about to head to class when Amber called out, "Hey, Zibby, come here for a sec."

"What's up?" Zibby reluctantly walked over to her.

"Now aren't you sorry you didn't want to be in my class anymore since there's such a mondo exciting event planned by *moi* to prepare for? And I must say, you need a lot of preparing," she smirked.

"Get real, Amber," Zibby shot back, now totally annoyed.

"This ball's not for real and you know it. There's no way you're going to pull it off!"

"Oh, didn't I tell you? I guess I didn't yet. My parents talked to Miss Cannon yesterday and that's going to be the theme of the of the sixth-grade dance. We're turning the dance into a ball! So I guess I *am* going to pull it off." She looked triumphantly at Zibby.

"You're what?" yelled Zibby. "You can't do that!"

"Yes, I can. I've already done it," stated Amber.

"That's not fair!" hollered Zibby.

"Get over it, Zibby. All the details have been worked out."

"I don't believe it! You're making this all up," sputtered Zibby.

"You wish, Zibby." Amber spun around on her metallic sandals and walked away.

This can't be true! It can't, thought Zibby. No way the school was going to let Amber steal the sixth-grade dance and replace it with some fancy ball! She couldn't wait to hear from Miss Cannon's lips that this was all just a big, fat figment of Amber's imagination.

CHAPTER 6

THE TERRIBLE TRUTH

Zibby ran to the classroom to find Miss Cannon and ask her about Amber's Crazy Plan, but the teacher was speaking to another kid ... right up until class started. Zibby, who'd had to work really hard to contain herself and not just burst in on the conversation, raised her hand the second she took her seat.

"Miss Cannon, about the sixth-grade dance – " she started to say.

"Oh yes, Zibby, thanks for the reminder. Everyone, I have a big announcement to make. Amber's parents called the school yesterday afternoon, and they're going to help us make this year's dance the best ever in the history of Lincoln Elementary. They have come up with an outstanding theme about a subject that is near and dear to my heart. So without any further ado, I am pleased to tell you that the name of this year's sixth-grade dance is the 'Mind Your Manners Ball'."

A few kids gasped and the boys all started frowning. But all of the girls in Amber's manners class grinned at each other and nodded excitedly.

So it was true! Zibby began to feel sick, as if her salmon-pickle sandwich wasn't agreeing very well with her. Amber had really taken over the sixth-grade dance.

Zibby sprung out of her seat. "Miss Cannon, I thought *we* were supposed to pick the theme – not have it chosen for us.

And I had a really good one I was going to suggest. After all, it's our dance – not Amber's parents' dance."

"That's true. But this year, Amber's parents overwhelmed us with their very generous offer and we just couldn't say no to taking the dance to another level. Now please, Zibby, sit down. And next time show some manners by raising your hand before speaking. After all, that *is* our theme."

Zibby sat down in her seat with an angry splat.

"As I was saying, this year's dance is truly going to be amazing. Amber's parents are going to donate all the food and drinks, and it's going to be first class all the way. They're providing us with china – from plates to an antique tea set since you'll all be drinking tea. And instead of eating greasy pizza as in past years, her parents are going to bring in catered finger sandwiches just like they serve at sophisticated country clubs."

Tea and finger sandwiches? Yuck, Zibby thought to herself. She'd take orange soda over tea any day. And the one time she ate a finger sandwich it had something in it called watercress that looked and tasted like clovers she'd find in her backyard. And Pizza Planet pizza wasn't greasy – and a lot better than some grass sandwich. Plus, she wanted The Everything – chocolate chips and all!

"And we're having a chocolate fountain, too!" called out Amber.

"Yes, we are," smiled Miss Cannon.

A few kids *oohed* and *aahed*.

"And, of course, since it's a manners ball, the girls will wear dresses and the boys will wear suits," Miss Cannon continued. "I know in years past, the dance was casual, but not this year. And if you don't have a dress or suit, don't worry. Amber's parents have a friend who owns a prop house filled with wonderful clothes, so you can borrow one for free."

"Oh no," Zibby muttered to herself. Now she was going to have to wear a *dress* to the dance? But she never wore dresses! Well, she did once, earlier in the year – a pink dress with lots of ruffles she called "Big Pink." But she only wore it because she *had to* for her Grandma Betty's birthday. This was a disaster!

But then she thought of something that might save her from Big Pink. She shot her hand up.

"What if you have a dress, but you don't want to wear it?"

"Well, I hope, in the spirit of the theme, you will, Zibby," Miss Cannon said firmly. "And I strongly recommend it."

"Oh," said Zibby, sinking down lower in her seat.

"And, since we are now dressing up, we need music to go with our sophisticated look, so Amber's parents are providing ballroom music for the dance as well," Miss Cannon added. "And Amber's aunt says she'll even teach you all how to waltz."

Zibby put her hands over her face in horror. There goes the jukebox! Adios to the Beatles music! Sayonara to the Eagles. Replaced by ballroom music and waltzing. The last fun thing about the dance was going, going, gone!

She dropped her hands from her face and then turned to glare at Amber. Amber just stared straight ahead as if she didn't notice. But Zibby could tell from the smug expression on Amber's face that she had.

"And I'm still running my manners classes for anyone who's interested," Amber piped up.

Amber hadn't raised her hand – yet again – but still Miss Cannon didn't reprimand *her*, Zibby noticed.

"That's right, and I hope you will all participate in Amber's classes," Miss Cannon wrapped up her announcement. "And now, it's finally time for us to get to work. So everyone, will you please turn to page thirty-five of your English workbooks so we can all get started?"

Zibby dutifully turned to page thirty-five, but hard as she tried, she couldn't concentrate on diagramming sentences. All she could think about was that this ball was the worst thing to ever happen in her entire sixth-grade year!

CHAPTER 7

BRAINWASHED BY THE BALL

"How can this be happening? Amber gets in trouble for giggling, and the next thing you know, she's hijacked the sixth-grade dance!" Zibby groused to Sarah and Gertrude at second recess.

"Outrageous!" agreed Gertrude. "A crime!"

"And so unfair," said Sarah. "Zibby, you never even got to suggest your theme."

"No one even likes the idea, except for Amber's manners minions," said Gertrude.

"Yeah, she may have brainwashed some of the girls, but did you see the boys' faces? The last thing they'd ever want to do is get all dressed up in some stuffy suit," said Zibby.

"But what can we do if Miss Cannon has made up her mind?" asked Sarah.

"Convince her to change it," answered Zibby. "If we can figure out a way, that is!"

Zibby wrinkled her forehead. Her mind wandered back to the other day when she was at the supermarket with her parents. A man had asked her mom to sign a petition against the school budget cuts the governor had suggested. The man said if they got enough signatures, the governor would have to listen to the people and change his mind. Well, if Zibby got enough signatures, Miss Cannon would have to listen to her!

"Hey, I have an idea!" she cried out. "We'll start a petition against this ball and get everyone to sign. Then we'll demand that the dance get changed back to the way it's always been ... and I can suggest my theme!"

"Do you really think that would work?" asked Gertrude.

"Of course," said Zibby. "This ball is so unpopular, when kids see the petition, they'll probably mob me."

She ripped a piece of paper out of her notebook and sat down at the table.

"Ouch!" Zibby felt something stab her upper thigh.

She looked down and realized she was wearing the same jean skirt she'd worn when she broke Amber's fish fork, and she still hadn't had her dad fix it.

"I'll get that taken care of soon, as soon as I take care of the dance!" she said to herself, adjusting the fork so it no longer dug into her.

On top of the paper she wrote: *Petition to Stop the Manners Ball. Sign Here*. Underneath she wrote the number "1" and her name.

"Now, you guys sign." She handed the sheet to her two friends, who quickly scribbled their names.

"Thanks. Now I'll be right back with tons of signatures!" said Zibby, and she ran out to the playground.

The first person she ran into was a girl named Bernice. Bernice had a unibrow and the only make-up she ever wore was her brother's Blistex, so Zibby figured she wasn't the type to go for a manners ball.

"Bernice! I have something for you to sign." She thrust the petition in front of Bernice's face.

"What?" asked Bernice, looking curious.

"I'm sure you'll agree with me that Amber can't just take our sixth-grade dance and turn it into some snobby ball, so I'm starting this petition to turn it back into the casual pizza night it's always been."

"But I'm allergic to cheese," said Bernice. "And pizza sauce makes me puke."

"Oh," Zibby faltered for a moment, then regrouped. "Okay then, so maybe you can't eat pizza, but do you really want to waltz around in some uncomfortable fancy dress and eat dainty little sandwiches all night?"

"No, but I heard something about a manicure and a pedicure, and I want those," Bernice mumbled, then flashed her ten fingers at Zibby. The tip of each nail was black with dirt.

"Hey, yours look just like mine! You're fine. You don't need a manicure," Zibby assured her.

"But wait! You should see my toes," said Bernice. She pulled off one of her tennis shoes and was starting to pull off her sock when Zibby was hit with a blast of Super-Stinky Feet Smell.

"That's okay. I get your point!" said Zibby, stepping quickly away. "Do not remove your sock. I repeat, do not remove your sock! I'll get someone else to sign my petition."

But the group of girls she approached next said no too. They couldn't pass up the chocolate fountain. The next crowd of girls wouldn't sign either. They'd just seen couples waltzing on some dance competition show, and couldn't wait to learn themselves. And two girls by the library blithered on about the free gowns they were going to borrow and how dare Zibby try to take away the ball from them.

Down, but not yet out, she jogged over to the soccer field. At least she knew she was guaranteed to get the boys' signatures! But even the boys rebuffed her.

"Um, sorry, tomboy," replied Matthew, her friend and best soccer buddy, when she asked him to sign. "Amber's parents called mine and talked them into the idea. My mom and dad are totally sold on it – they think it will be good for me – and I can't go against my parents."

"They called my parents too," mumbled a boy named Zane, frowning.

"Mine too," admitted still another boy, Drew.

Out of the boys, all but three had received Amber's Parents' "Summons to the Ball," and they were the only ones left to sign the petition.

So it was that by the end of lunch, instead of the dozens of signatures she'd expected to collect, Zibby had a Grand Total of six.

She looked down at the petition, and then crumpled it in her hand. *Six signatures isn't going to change Miss Cannon's mind, not at all*, she thought as she threw it in the trash can. Like it or not, she was stuck with the ball. What was she going to do now?

CHAPTER 8

ZIBBY'S BIG IDEA

"It's so unfair!" she complained for about the millionth time that day, this time after school to Anthony after telling him the whole story of Amber's Sixth Grade Dance Takeover. Her dad was out of town on a business trip for a few days, so she'd asked Anthony to help her save Amber's fish fork since he was good at fixing things too. She was leaning over Anthony as he sat at his desk bending back the fork prongs with pliers.

"This 'ball' does sound pretty uncool," he agreed. "There" – he straightened the last prong – "that looks pretty good, doesn't it?" He held up the fork for her inspection.

Zibby looked at it carefully.

"Thanks. This should meet with her highness' approval." Zibby stuck the fork back in her pocket and made a mental note to return it to Amber.

"So what do *you* think I should do?" she asked her brother.

"About Amber's dance?" he asked. He leaned back in his chair. "I dunno. Not go?"

"No way! It's my dance too. I just want to make it fun ... somehow!"

She picked up a piece of paper from Anthony's desk and began fiddling with it as she pondered her problem. When she looked down at it, the title on the paper, "Opposite Day

45

Schedule," caught her attention.

"Hey, what's this?" she asked.

"The class schedule for tomorrow. Twice a year we have an Opposite Day that the teachers plan 'to keep us on our toes,' they say. So tomorrow, I start with my last class and end with what's normally my first class."

"Hmm," she said. "Interesting idea. Doing the opposite." She flopped down on Anthony's bed. "I wish I could do the opposite of Amber's ball," she sighed. She thought for a few seconds more, and just then she got the spark of one of her Very Good Ideas that quickly blossomed into a full-on Very Good Idea.

"I know what I'm going to do!" she yelled. "Sarah, Gertrude, and I can have an Opposite Ball. We'll go to the dance, but once we get there, we'll do the opposite of what Amber's planned. We'll wear the opposite of formal clothes, eat the opposite of finger sandwiches, stuff like that!"

"Very creative," Anthony nodded.

"But," Zibby furrowed her brow, "calling it an Opposite Ball isn't quite right. It's more like we're going to throw..." she stared off into space while waiting for inspiration to strike.

"An anti-ball?" suggested Anthony.

"Yes, much better," said Zibby. "I like the sound of that!"

She gave her brother a big hug. "Thanks so much, Anthony! You just saved the sixth-grade dance!"

"Yeah, I am pretty awesome," he smiled, "even though the idea was yours. But I do rock for fixing that fishy fork or whatever it was. Now get out of here, will you? I've got tons of bio homework."

"I am *so* out of here," Zibby said. She ran out of his room and across the hall to her own, her head already swimming with all the anti-ball activities they could do at Amber's ball. She grabbed a sheet of paper, and after much thought, produced the following list:

Amber's Ball	Zibby's Anti-ball
Dress formal.	Dress casual ... and even better, off-the-wall weird! (Note to self: Find striped tights; borrow a tutu from Sarah?)
Arrive in a limo.	Arrive on a scooter.
Walk down the red carpet.	Walk around the red carpet.
Eat finger sandwiches and drink tea.	Get pizza delivered. (Note to self: Check piggy bank to see how to pay for it.) Soft drinks would be awesome too.
Chocolate fountain.	Gummy worm mountain.
Play old fogey music.	Play rock and roll on my iPod. (Note to self: Borrow Anthony's new speakers since they sound really good, plus they are loud!)
Fancy china.	No plates at all – we'll eat with our hands (who needs plates anyway?).
Waltzing.	Ummm ... definitely no walzing!

When she finished, she was so pumped, she kicked an invisible soccer ball across the room as if she was scoring the winning goal in a game. *Oh this is gonna be great!* She couldn't wait to tell Sarah and Gertrude her plan, which, in her mind, she was already calling "The Red Carpet Revolt."

* * *

"I have to tell you something," she said as she ran up to Sarah on the blacktop the next morning. "And where's Gertrude? I need to tell her too."

"She's not here yet," said Sarah, her eyes wandering over to Amber, who was in the middle of an early morning headband demonstration for her the girls in her manners class.

"When you put the headband on, make sure your hair doesn't pooch up in front, or you'll look like a real dork," Amber was saying authoritatively as she slid a headband on. "Practice at recess, and we can discuss it more at lunch."

"Sarah, what are you doing?" asked Zibby sharply. Why was Sarah listening to Amber?

"Oh, nothing," said Sarah quickly. "It's just that the headband is kinda cute. I wonder where Amber got it."

"Forget about the headband," commanded Zibby. "I've got something really important to tell you guys – oh, and there's Gertrude! Let's go meet up with her."

The two girls walked over to Gertrude, and Zibby quickly filled them both in on her Big Plan.

"So, what do you think?" she asked when she finished talking.

"It's totally rad," said Gertrude excitedly. "And I have

tons of funky clothes I found at *Déjà You* the other day that I can wear."

"Cool," smiled Zibby.

"Oh, and my dad knows the manager of Pizza Planet, so I bet he can get us a good deal on the pizzas, too. And if we all throw in our allowances, we'll have enough," added Gertrude. "Last time I checked, I had about $16."

"Great – and I counted my money last night and I have $21. With a discount, that should be enough for several large Everythings," said Zibby excitedly.

She turned to Sarah, who was being noticeably quiet.

"What about you? You haven't said anything yet."

"Oh ... well ... the idea's ... um ... good, and I've got some money I can give for the pizza, too," said Sarah. But she didn't sound very enthusiastic.

"Is something wrong?" asked Zibby.

"Not really, it's just that I did sort of want to wear that dress my mom got me," Sarah admitted. But then she smiled. "But it's okay. I don't like this whole Manners Ball any more than you do."

"Good, so we're set, then," said Zibby, happy both Sarah and Gertrude were on board for the Red Carpet Revolt. "We'll figure out the rest of the details later!"

"Oh one more thing," said Sarah, looking worried all of a sudden. "We're not going to get in trouble for this, are we?"

"Nah, I don't think so," said Zibby. But the truth was she hadn't even thought about that until now. However, she didn't think it seemed likely.

"Miss Cannon didn't say we *had* to dress up. She just recommended it," Zibby said. Okay, she admitted to herself,

Miss Cannon did recommend it *strongly*, but there was a big difference between recommending something and making it a rule. "And how can she get mad if we bring in more food and supplies?" she asked. "The school's always asking for donations of everything."

"That's true," said Sarah. But she still looked worried.

"Is there something else bothering you?" asked Zibby.

"Well, now I'm wondering about Amber," Sarah said. "How's she going to feel about our anti-ball?"

"She'll never know!" said Zibby. "It's our secret – we can't let her find out in case she tries to stop us."

"But she'll find out for sure at the ball," said Sarah. "And then don't you think she'll be mad or upset ... or something?"

"Oh," Zibby frowned. She hadn't thought about *that* either. But now that Sarah mentioned it, she didn't think it would be a problem.

"She probably won't get angry – since when does she care what we do, anyway?" Zibby replied. "Plus it's not like we're doing anything to hurt her ball. We're just trying to have fun."

"If anything, she'll probably laugh at us or make us feel like we're stupid," said Gertrude. "Not that I care."

"Me neither," said Zibby a little too loud as she often did when she felt strongly about things. "So, are you both in?" she asked, feeling as if all the issues had been talked through now.

"You know it," said Gertrude.

Sarah, however, didn't answer. Her eyes had drifted back to Amber.

"Oh no. Are you *still* worried about something?" asked Zibby.

"No, I'm fine now. It's just that I suddenly got an idea

myself." She looked at Zibby. "So at the ball, we're going to do the opposite of everything Amber has planned, right?"

"Yep," said Zibby happily.

"But if you *really* want to do the opposite, don't you have to know exactly *what* Amber is planning to do at the ball?" asked Sarah.

"We do – she already told us and so did Miss Cannon," said Zibby.

"Yeah, but who knows what else she's got planned at the big ball? Don't we have to be ready to do the opposite of whatever else she's teaching the girls to do?"

"Oh," said Zibby. "I didn't think of that. But how do we do that?"

"There's only one way. We have to take her classes in order to get the full scoop!" Sarah's voice rose.

"What?" yelled Zibby. That was the last thing she ever wanted to do – endure more of Amber's classes!

"It's the only way. How else can we plan a revolt if we don't know exactly what we're revolting against?" Sarah asked practically.

"So, you mean, we take her classes and pretend to go along with them, but in reality we're *really* gathering material for the revolt, doing a sort of etiquette espionage, just like those undercover cops on TV?" asked Gertrude.

"Exactly," Sarah nodded.

"I think Sarah has a good point," Gertrude said to Zibby. "Otherwise we may miss a lot of things."

"So *you* think we should take Amber's classes too?" asked Zibby, starting to warm up to the idea since both Sarah and Gertrude thought it was a good one.

"As painful as that sounds, I do," said Gertrude. "And we'll keep a list of all the new anti-ball activities we think of!"

"Well, if it's for the sake of the Red Carpet Revolt, let's do it," Zibby conceded somewhat reluctantly.

"Hurray!" said Gertrude and Sarah together.

But as she walked to class a little later, her stomach gave a little lurch. She *could* tolerate a few more of Amber's classes, couldn't she?

CHAPTER 9

SMILE FOR THE CAMERA

"Work it, Zibby; work it! Pretend you're a model. Or a movie star. Somebody famous. Just not you!" yelled Amber.

It was lunch the following week, and Zibby was indeed back in Amber's manners class, which had grown even bigger and now included sixteen girls. The lesson for the day was "The Red Carpet Walk & Wave." Amber had lined a walkway with backpacks, and girls were taking turns strutting through it pretending to be on a real red carpet, which, Amber promised, would be delivered to the cafeteria in time for the ball.

Zibby was taking a solo spin down the pretend carpet, but walking "like a model or a movie star" didn't come easy to her.

"Come on, Zibby, get some bounce in your step!" yelled Amber. "Now that you've smartened up and have decided to take my classes again, at least *try*!"

"I *am* trying," said Zibby, insulted, because for once, she really was.

"Stop now and do the wave," commanded Amber.

Zibby quit walking. She cupped her hand and slowly turned it from side to side like she'd seen girls do on parade floats.

"No, not like that!" Amber snapped. "Like this." She gave a little wave with her fingers. "*This* is the movie star wave!"

"*Okay*," said Zibby testily. She raised her hand and did what she thought was quite a good wave.

"No, that's not it either," hissed Amber.

"How about like this then?" asked Zibby. She placed her two hands on top of her head as if making Mickey Mouse ears and wiggled her fingers.

"You're hopeless, Zibby," sighed Amber. "Someone else get up here, quick!" She looked around.

"You – Grace – now!"

But Grace didn't do much better than Zibby. After Amber berated her because she "clumped down the runway like a cow," Grace looked as if she was about to cry.

"Looks like the Queen of Mean is getting even meaner," whispered Zibby to Gertrude.

"Can we say *Cruella de Vil*?" asked Gertrude.

After the lesson was over, Zibby couldn't help but complain to Sarah. "Not only was the lesson stupid, it was a waste of time because I didn't get any new material for the anti-ball! I already knew she was going to have everyone walk down a red carpet."

"That's not true," said Sarah. "You learned about the movie star wave. And I loved your silly Mickey Mouse wave. You can add *that* to our list!"

"That's true," said Zibby. She pulled out her notebook and scribbled away. "I sure hope learning that one little tidbit for our underground revolt was worth giving up my entire lunch for."

Zibby regretted her sacrificed lunch the next day too, as she sat through Amber's "Smile for the Camera" class. A friend of Amber's dad, a professional photographer, was going to take photos of the girls the night of the ball, and Amber wanted to make sure they all knew how to "smile with style."

"Relax your mouth, and don't show too many teeth!" Amber criticized Gertrude.

"No gummy smiles either," she reprimanded Lyla.

"And don't forget your eyes, peeps! Make *them* smile too!" she added to everyone.

"How do you smile with your eyes?" Zibby asked Katherine, who was standing next to her.

"I don't have a clue," Katherine shrugged her shoulders, looking stressed. "Her classes are getting really, really hard! I don't know what she's talking about half the time and I never seem to do anything right."

"Leave it to Amber to think of 'smiling eyes'," said Zibby, and then she crossed her eyes.

"Oh Zibby!" Katherine smiled, and then, when she was sure Amber wasn't looking, she crossed her eyes, too.

Well, at least I've found another anti-ball activity to add to the list, Zibby consoled herself, writing down "crossing your eyes for the photographer."

And after that day, a curious thing happened. She almost began to enjoy Amber's lessons. Because she knew by the end of each one, she'd find something else that would make the Underground Red Carpet Revolt even better! Her list of anti-ball activities was growing satisfyingly longer and longer!

After Amber's "Perfect Posture Now" lesson where Zibby had to practice walking with her shoulders back by balancing a stack of *Celeb Chat* magazines on her head, Zibby added to the list, "Be comfy – and if you slump a little, so what?"

After Amber's "Drink Tea Like a Debutante" class, where Zibby learned to drink her tea in itsy bitsy sips, she wrote "Take satisfying slurps!"

And after Amber's "How to Be a Dainty Chewer" lecture, Zibby scribbled, "Cram as much pizza into your mouth as possible."

"This isn't as bad as I thought," she said to herself. But then came Amber's next lesson. And if Zibby had known how *that* was going to turn out, she never would have gone undercover in the first place!

"Who's she?" Zibby whispered to Gertrude and Sarah at the start of Amber's next class, pointing to a short woman with red hair in a lime green pantsuit who was standing next to Amber.

"No clue," replied Gertrude. Sarah shrugged her shoulders to say she didn't know either.

But the secret of the mysterious redhead in the green pantsuit was soon revealed.

"Hey, everyone, give a shout-out to my amazingly awesome Aunt Bev!" Amber called to the class. "She's a former beauty queen, like I've told you, and she's here to help us today. She's going to teach us how to waltz. So thank you, Aunt Bev! And by the way, you may all call her that, too – Aunt Bev!"

"Thank you, Aunt Bev," called out several of the girls enthusiastically.

No thank you, no thank you at all, thought Zibby, definitely Not Happy to have to learn the waltz. She was also surprised by Amber's aunt. She looked kind of regular – not like a beauty queen at all. Which, actually, was a point in Aunt Bev's favor, as far as Zibby was concerned. A big one. She looked at Aunt Bev, and before she knew what she was doing, she gave Amber's aunt a big smile.

"Oh, I can see I've got a waltzer out there," Aunt Bev beamed at her. "You" – she pointed to Zibby. "You come out here and be my partner. You and I are going to demonstrate the graceful ballet of feelings, movement, and pure beauty that is known as the Viennese Waltz."

"What?" Zibby stared at her in terror, unable to move.

CHAPTER 10

A LESSON TO FORGET

There was just one little problem with Aunt Bev's suggestion. Zibby couldn't dance. At all! She was a total klutz. It was weird because she was so coordinated on the soccer field. But not on the dance floor!

"No, not me," she cried out.

"Yes, you!" insisted Aunt Bev. "Don't be shy, hon! I know your inner waltzer is just waiting to come out. Now get on out here on the count of three – one, two, three!" Then she gave a short burst of laughter. "One, two, three; get it? That's the step of the waltz, but it's also how fast I want you to get out here. And I mean it. Get out here right now!" she yelled.

"Okay," Zibby reluctantly stood up and slowly walked over to her.

"So what's your name?" Aunt Bev asked her.

"Zibby."

"Zibby? That's not a name, hon. Your real name."

"Elizabeth."

"And your middle name?"

"Um ... Mildred," Zibby said softly.

"What?" roared Aunt Bev.

"MILDRED, I said," Zibby spat out.

A few of the girls who didn't know Zibby very well giggled. Zibby didn't really advertise that her middle name was as old-lady sounding as Mildred. Personally, Zibby didn't mind her middle name. But she well understood that to most sixth graders, it was something to make fun of, and for that reason, she didn't run around telling everyone what it was.

"So Elizabeth Mildred, please stand facing me and hold out your arms."

Zibby did as she was told.

"Now, you will be the girl, and I will be the boy. Because of course, when you really waltz, you waltz with boys. Now place your right hand on my shoulder and hold my other hand like this." Aunt Bev put the death grip on Zibby as if she was never going to let go.

Zibby really didn't think any boy in the class would ever get so close to a girl, and she considered telling Aunt Bev waltzing would never work for the sixth-grade dance, but the next thing she knew, Aunt Bev was barking out more dancing commands.

"Step back with your right foot, then step back and to the left with your left foot. Then slide your right foot over to your left. Try those three steps," commanded Aunt Bev.

"Now?" asked Zibby.

"Now," nodded Aunt Bev.

"One, two, three," Aunt Bev counted as Zibby attempted the steps.

"Well, hon, you're three for three," Aunt Bev said when they were done.

"You mean I did it right?" asked Zibby.

"No, you stepped on my toes three for three steps!"

"Sorry," apologized Zibby. She'd been way too focused on her own feet to notice where Aunt Bev's were, and maybe she *had* bumped into them a little, but not that much.

A few girls snickered.

"Bigfoot," someone whispered – someone who sounded like Amber.

Zibby shot her the evil eye. And Camille too, in case Amber's snarky comments were contagious.

Aunt Bev took a deep breath and then smiled. "Let's try again. Now, step forward with your left foot, step forward and to the right with your right foot, then slide your left foot over to your … ouchamagoucha!" she yelled.

This time there was no mistaking what Zibby had done. During the slide, she slid too far and landed big time on Aunt Bev's toes.

"Dickens-chickens, that hurt!" Aunt Bev took off her black pump and rubbed her toes.

"I am so sorry, again," Zibby apologized.

"Hon, I don't mean to be unkind, but are you just one of those uncoordinated girls?" she asked.

Someone laughed. Zibby shot the crowd a look.

"No, I am very coordinated! I play soccer. And I'm good."

"Oh, well, I'm sure you are, hon," said Aunt Bev, putting her shoe back on slowly. "But I think right now, it's time for me to get another partner. Why don't you just sit over there and watch for a while."

Zibby nodded, then quickly sat down at a table. While she was relieved not to have to waltz anymore, she couldn't help but feel insulted over Aunt Bev's last comment about her not being coordinated. After all the embarrassment of trying to dance, this final one was just too much.

Amber's "Smile for the Paparazzi" class had been painful,

the "Red Carpet Walk & Wave" class woefully awful, and the "Tea Drinking Session" a big bore, but this "Ballroom Dancing with Aunt Bev" had been humiliating with a capital "H." And, she hadn't even gotten an anti-ball activity out of it since she already knew there was no way she was ever gonna dance the waltz at the ball! Maybe she couldn't stick out this Etiquette Espionage after all.

CHAPTER 11

UNDERCOVER, AGAIN

"Yuck," Zibby said to herself the next day as she dragged herself back to Amber's class.

If this lesson went even half as bad as yesterday's – even one-fourth as bad – she was going to quit the spy business! Gertrude and Sarah could continue on with the undercover work without her.

But when she arrived at Amber's table, a miracle happened. Amber announced that she'd taught them everything she knew, and that they were all ready for their "debutante ball debut." So instead of toughing out another of Amber's classes, she went out to play soccer with the boys.

"Yippee!" said Zibby to Sarah and Gertrude later that day at second recess as the girls talked under the shade of a pepper tree.

"Excellent news," agreed Gertrude. "I've had it with her and her silly manners!"

But Sarah almost seemed a little sad.

"That raspberry tea she served the other day was really good. And I did sort of like the waltz, even though I hated the way Aunt Bev put you on the spot, Zibby."

"Freedom," sang out Zibby. "That's all I have to say. And now we can all just focus on having a ton of fun at the dance."

"Hey, shhh," Gertrude suddenly whispered. "Better keep

it down – someone's coming."

Zibby turned around to see Katherine and Grace walking toward them.

"Hi," said Grace in a small voice, her shoulders slumped.

"Yeah, hi," said Katherine. She didn't look happy either and she had circles under her eyes.

"What's wrong with you two? You seem pretty down," Sarah asked, concerned.

"I'm just tired. Amber's lessons have wiped me out," complained Grace.

"It's taking so much time," groused Katherine. "I borrowed a dress from that prop house, and now Amber wants me to come over to her house to accessorize tonight. But I've got Girl Scouts and my Future Mathematicians of America meeting, so how am I going to fit it all in?"

"And you should hear what she told me," griped Grace. "When I showed her *my* dress, she told me it made my elbows look fat and that I should hide them – with super-long gloves! But how can elbows even look fat. Can you tell me that?"

"Don't listen to her! She's gone psycho over her ball," said Zibby, shaking her head in disbelief.

"She's turning into one of those brides you see on those TV shows who go crazy. What do they call them – Bridezillas?" asked Gertrude. "I guess she'd be a Debutantzilla."

"At least it will be over soon. The ball's this Saturday, which is only a few days away," shrugged Grace.

"If we make it, that is," added Katherine.

Just then, from across the blacktop, Amber's voice boomed, "Hey you guys, get over here."

Grace turned around to look at Amber. She was wagging a

finger as if to say, "Move it on over here."

"Now what does she want?" asked Grace. "I hope it's not any more elbow slimming tips she got on *brainlessbeautytips. com*."

"Come on, we'd better go before she gets even more mad or something." Katherine took Grace's arm and the two girls went hurrying off toward Amber.

"Those poor things," said Sarah. "I feel so bad for them. And for all the girls. They don't seem as if they're having any fun at all."

"I feel bad for them too," said Zibby. "But in a way, I also don't. Because if they hadn't gone all gaga over the ball in the first place, we'd still be having our normal dance and everyone would be happy."

"But they didn't know that Amber would turn into such an evil event-planning control freak," said Gertrude.

"I guess that's true," said Zibby. The girls couldn't have known what they were getting themselves into. Boy, was she glad, however, that she didn't have to go along with any of Amber's etiquette essentials anymore!

But then, Amber yelled across the blacktop again. And this time, she was calling *their* names. "Zibby, Gertrude, Sarah, you guys too. Over here now!"

"Oh no, " groaned Zibby. "Can we just ignore her?"

"I don't see how," said Sarah. "Come on, let's just got see what she has to say."

Slowly the girls walked over to where Amber was holding court in front of all the girls who had attended her lessons.

"Now that we're all here, I have a special announcement," Amber smiled. "I just got off the phone with my mom, and I have a new exciting announcement! When I first mentioned my ball, I told you all I'd get you mani-pedis and get your hair done. So I've arranged a pre-ball party for all of us. As a special present from *moi* to you. Wasn't that nice of me?"

"Yes, Amber, thank you," several of the girls replied – but a bit mechanically, Zibby thought.

"I expect you all at my house at 3:00 pm sharp this Saturday. Don't be late, and make sure you come wearing your dresses. We'll spend the afternoon getting our hair and make-up done, and getting mani-pedis, and then the limo will pick us up at 5:30 pm. It will take us to Matthew's house, where a few of the boys will be, and then onto the school by 6:00 pm for the ball. My dad and uncle will be at the school helping Miss Cannon set up, but my mom and my Aunt Bev will be running beauty stations at my house. In fact, I've put together a little schedule to make sure you all get your primp time."

She took a stack of papers out of her backpack and started passing them around.

Zibby looked down at her copy and saw she was slated for hair at 3:30 pm, makeup at 4:00 pm, and a mani-pedi at 5:00 pm.

Ha! She thought to herself. *Like that's gonna happen.* She was so going to ditch this pre-ball party. It had nothing to do with the Revolt, and therefore nothing to do with her! But she didn't want to cause a stink right then, so she figured she'd tell Amber later.

Zibby wandered over to the trash can at the edge of the blacktop and was about to throw away the schedule when Sarah stopped her. "What are you doing?" she asked.

"Throwing this stupid schedule away. I don't need it. You

don't either. Or Gertrude."

"But wait a minute! Because if we're really going undercover, then we've got to go undercover the entire way," said Sarah.

"What do you mean?" asked Zibby, getting a bad feeling.

"We've got to go to the pre-party too. Otherwise Amber would get suspicious about why we weren't there and start wondering what we were up to, and it might blow our entire cover!"

"I don't think she'd even notice if we weren't there, do you?" asked Zibby.

"Yes – she notices everything. You know that. In fact, if we didn't show up, she'd probably call us and hound us and make us come over. And then we'd be stuck at the last minute all trying to come up with lies."

"But I'm a good liar," declared Zibby.

"Well, I'm not! And what if, let's say, Anthony got on the phone and let our plans slip?"

"I'll tell him not to tell anyone!"

"It's too complicated. Too risky. I think Gertrude's even told her parents about it, and they could tip off Amber too. Let's just all go and keep the charade a little bit longer. For the sake of the Revolt, we've got to go."

Zibby sighed. Maybe Sarah had a point. Maybe it was safer just to go to the pre-party. Even though the thought of it was Horrifyingly Horrible!

"So let me get this straight – I have to get my hair and nails done – and my make-up, too?" Zibby asked, gagging at the thought of the Groovy Grapilicious lip gloss and gross pancake makeup she was forced to wear in the school play earlier in the year.

"No, I don't think so. Even if Amber did put you on the schedule, she knows you're not into that. You can probably get away with not actually doing any of it."

"That's a relief," said Zibby. "But I'd still have to wear a dress, wouldn't I?" She cringed at the idea of putting Big Pink on again.

"Yes, but only for the pre-party," said Sarah.

"Well, when do we change our clothes then?" asked Zibby, feeling put out.

"We could put our crazy clothes on under our dresses and then change right when we get there," said Sarah.

"But I was going to ask you if I could wear one of your tutus and also a feather boa, if I can find one, and a funny hat too. What about those? They won't fit under my dress."

"Hmm," Sarah thought for a moment. "We'll each take a bag with us for all that extra stuff. See? It'll all work out. No problem."

"This is a huge change in plans," Zibby shook her head. "What about the limo? We're supposed to take scooters, not the limo, to the ball!"

"That's true. But you know, I hear it has a mini-fridge, so it won't be that bad. It might even be fun," said Sarah. "Now, listen, I'm going to go tell Gertrude about the new plan. And don't worry, Zibby, you'll be fine," she said before hurrying away.

"Fine?" yelped Zibby, thinking, *yeah, right!*

The whole reason she planned the Revolt was so she wouldn't have to follow any of Amber's red carpet rules, and here she was following even more of them yet again! Just

when she solved one problem another cropped up. Just trying
to make the sixth-grade dance fun ... as it should have been in
the first place ... was sure getting complicated.

CHAPTER 12

PLENTY OF PINK

"Where is it?" Zibby yelled as she frantically pawed through her closet. It was D-Day – Saturday afternoon before the ball – and she was desperately trying to find Big Pink.

The last few days had been a whirlwind of Red Carpet Revolt preparations. She'd rounded up the pizza money, ordered four large Everythings, as well as a few jumbo bottles of soda, and arranged for them to be delivered at the cafeteria at 6:30 pm, a half hour after the dance started. She'd bought a bag of gummy worms to dump out next to the chocolate fountain. She'd downloaded an awesome selection of songs on her iPod, and she borrowed Anthony's speakers.

She'd also picked up the tutu from Sarah, found a feather boa from her mom's closet, and borrowed a leprechaun hat from Anthony, which he wore last Halloween. Then she'd put everything in a large bag.

And at the last minute, she thought of yet another fun thing to do as she entered the dance, one that fit in with the theme *she* wanted, so she'd had to work out all those details too.

Now all that was left to do was get ready for the pre-party, which she couldn't do until she found her dumb dress! She reached into the very back corner of the closet, and there it was, half falling off a hanger, wrinkled, and looking very ... pink.

"Oh well," she consoled herself. "I won't have to wear it for long."

She already had on as many of her wacky clothes as she felt would fit under the dress – an old ratty T-shirt, frayed jean skirt, and crazy tights. (Luckily, Big Pink came down to her ankles so she could get away with the tights.) She stepped into Big Pink, then tried to pull up the zipper. But with the extra clothes on, the dress was too tight for her to zip up all the way on her own.

She flung open her bedroom door. "Mo-om," she bellowed. "I need some help, please!"

"Coming," her mom called from the kitchen.

Zibby hadn't told her mom about the Revolt and had asked Anthony not to tell either, just in case her mom didn't like the idea. So she quickly made up a little fib about why she was wearing a shirt.

"This dress is super-itchy," she announced. "So I'm wearing a shirt underneath. But now it's too tight for me to zip up on my own. Can you please help?" She turned around so her back was facing her mom.

Her mom sounded surprised. "It's itchy? But it's satin."

"It is! Mom! Totally!" she said loudly.

"Okay, Zibby," her mom sighed as she zipped her up. "Now, when you get to Amber's, will you tell her parents 'thank you'? I wouldn't have picked a manners ball as the theme for sixth grade, but I know they've worked very hard on it and spent a lot of their own money. So please let them know how much you appreciate it."

"Will do," said Zibby, sending her mom a very strong "Now please go so I can finish getting dressed on my own" vibe.

"Okay, well, if I don't see you before Mrs. Shroeder comes" – Sarah's mom was driving them – "have a great time," her mom said.

"I will," said Zibby. Of that she was sure. If she could just get ready!

Once her mom was gone, Zibby slammed the door shut, and then looked at herself in the mirror. Except for a bit of bulkiness around the middle of the dress you couldn't even tell she had all the extra clothes on. Amber would never suspect a thing.

She bent over to touch her toes to make sure that if she ever had to lean over, her tights wouldn't show – they didn't! – when she felt something prick her stomach. What was that? She stood up and felt the outline of something skinny and sharp.

Oh no, the fish fork! It was still in her pocket! She'd still never remembered to return it to Amber.

Oh well, I'll give it to her tonight, she thought.

Next she ran a comb quickly through her hair – she'd bring a ponytail holder for later – and then she put on a pair of athletic socks and her high-tops. She knew that to stay in "ball lovers' character," she should be wearing some sandals, but she just couldn't make herself go that deep undercover.

Sarah's mom picked her up at 2:45 pm, and Zibby piled into the way-back of the mini-van with Sarah and Gertrude. Sarah was wearing a pretty white dress and Gertrude had on a velvet dress she'd bought at *Déjà You* that cost $9.99. The girls did a quick wardrobe check to make sure none of their clothes could be see through or under their dresses, then they checked out each others' "props" in their bags.

"Love it," said Gertrude, admiring Zibby's feather boa.

"This is great," Zibby exclaimed to Sarah about a pair of bright green leg warmers she'd brought to change into.

"We are so going to shake things up tonight," smiled Gertrude.

"We're making sixth grade dance history, that's for sure!" said Zibby.

When they arrived at Amber's house, they found the living room had been turned into a beauty salon. Amber's mom stood behind a chair curling Camille's hair. Aunt Bev sat at a small table polishing Katherine's nails. Another woman, who Zibby didn't know, was putting make-up on Lyla.

"Welcome to my own little BC," said Amber, appearing from her bedroom wearing a pink, fluffy robe. Her hair was piled on top of her head in a bun.

"Huh?" asked Zibby.

"Beauty Central, duh," snapped Amber. Then she noticed Zibby was wearing high-tops.

"Real high-fashion shoes, Zibby," she smirked. "Good choice for a ball."

"Thanks," Zibby smiled, thinking that while it might not be a good choice for a ball, it certainly was a good one for an anti-ball.

"All right! Who's up next for a manicure and pedicure? I'm ready for my 3:05 appointment!" said Aunt Bev.

"It's me!" yelled Sarah, rushing over. She ran over so quickly in fact, Zibby couldn't help but say to Gertrude, "I really get the feeling she likes all this. What do you think?"

"Could be. She sure didn't hesitate."

"Not at all," agreed Zibby.

She couldn't, however, say the same thing for herself. When it was time for her 3:30 hair appointment with Amber's mom, she smiled and told Amber's mom that she'd already spent all day working on her hair.

"You have?" asked Amber's mom, looking doubtful.

"Yes I have. It's that new messy look that's in, where you look like you haven't combed it for days, but you've really been brushing it for hours," she said, hoping her white lies would get her out of a hairstyling.

"I haven't heard about that, but it looks nice on you. Very natural," Amber's mom smiled.

Zibby was also able to duck the make-up station by running into the kitchen and chatting with Lyla and Katherine during the time of her appointment. And she thought she was going to be able to get out of the mani-pedi appointment by sitting outside in Amber's backyard petting her dog Zorro, but Aunt Bev came out to find her.

"Elizabeth Mildred, hon, you're up. Now you're not going to go running away on me, are you?"

"Oh, no," replied Zibby, even though, of course she wished she could.

"Then get on over here," Aunt Bev nodded toward the house, "and let me take care of those nails!"

Reluctantly Zibby followed her inside.

"Dickens-chickens! Ever had a manicure before?" Aunt Bev asked as they settled in their seats and she got a good look at Zibby's nails.

"No," said Zibby.

"Well, your nails are going to be a challenge for me, but when I get done with you, you're going to look like the belle of the ball."

More like the rebel of the ball, Zibby thought to herself with a grin.

She sat there for a while, trying not to squirm as Aunt Bev buffed and filed. Then Zibby asked, "So, I hear you were a beauty queen. What kind?"

"Years ago, I was the Kumquat Queen. It may not sound like much to you, but in the town in Florida where I grew up, which is the kumquat capital of the states, let me tell you, it was a real big deal."

"I'm sure it was," said Zibby politely, wondering what a kumquat was exactly since she didn't think she'd ever eaten one. Was it that orange fruit that looked like a small, oval tangerine? Or was that a guava?

She was thinking so hard, trying to conjure up a mental picture of a kumquat, that she didn't even notice that Aunt Bev had started painting the nails on her left hand pink.

Zibby snatched her hand back and gasped. " I wanted clear – if anything at all!"

"No clear for you. This color is called Pleasing Pink, and it matches your dress perfectly." Aunt Bev pulled Zibby's hand back, and then quickly finished polishing her nails.

"There, we're done!" Aunt Bev said cheerfully.

"I don't have to get a pedicure now too, do I?" asked Zibby. Having ten Pleasing Pink fingernails was bad enough, but having 10 matching toenails was Unthinkable!

"Hon, that manicure took so long, there isn't any time for your feet. But since you're wearing tennies," she glanced down at Zibby's feet, "it won't matter anyway."

"That's right!" agreed Zibby, relieved.

Zibby plunked herself down in the chair Aunt Bev demanded she sit in to let her nails dry, and looked at her nails again. Boy, did she hate them. Really hate them. Not only that, the polish felt suffocating – it was as if her fingertips couldn't breathe.

"My nails need to be free," she said to herself. She looked around, and grabbed a box of Kleenex off a nearby table, then started wiping the polish off her nails. But only some of it came off. Still, a little bit of streaky pink polish was better than a lot of pink polish, so she breathed easier ... and so did her fingertips!

Just then, Amber entered the room. She'd changed from her robe into a black strapless gown and high heels.

Wow, thought Zibby. *She looks like a living Barbie doll* – and that *wasn't* a compliment.

Her "peeps," however, thought otherwise.

"You look amazing," cried Camille.

"Ditto," squealed Savannah.

Amber, however, didn't seem happy with the comments. She looked tense, and instead of saying "thank you," she began snapping orders. "Camille, you need more lip gloss. Savannah, fix your strap. It's sagging."

Just then her rhinestone-encrusted pink cell phone rang. She thrust it up to hear ear, nodded, and shouted, "Copy that!" and slammed the phone shut. She then looked at the girls and yelled, "We've got to snap to it! That was the limo driver. He's just pulled up outside the house and is waiting for us. And we've also got to pick up the boys. So let's get moving – *double pronto, people!*" and she ran out of the room, practically knocking over Katherine.

"Talk about pre-ball stress – Amber is losing it," Zibby said to herself, as she began to walk outside. But before she got out the door, she was hit with her own pre-ball stress because she realized she'd left her bag with all her gear somewhere inside.

"Oh no," she cried out, turning and running back inside the house. She looked at the hair station. And then at the nail beauty station. Where was her bag? She ran outside, and finally found it lying by the back door. She must have left it there when she was petting Zorro.

She grabbed the bag, rushed back inside through the house, and flew out the front door. But when she got there, the limo was already gone!

CHAPTER 13

ZIBBY, UNZIPPED!

I can't believe they left without me, was Zibby's first thought. Her second was, *I've got to hurry up and get to the ball!*

She ran back inside the house looking for Amber's mom or the other women who'd been tending the beauty stations to ask if they could give her a ride, but the house was empty. They must have gone along in the limo too.

"Now what?" she asked herself. Maybe her parents could drive her to the school. She called home, but no one answered. She thought about calling them on their cell phones, but quickly vetoed it. They'd freak out and think something was really wrong.

Just then her eyes fell on a scooter that someone had leaned against the house along the driveway. *Hey, maybe I can scooter over to the ball as I had originally planned*, she figured. The school wasn't that far and at least she had her tennis shoes on.

She grabbed the scooter, and with a push from her right foot, she was off! She careened down the driveway and onto the street, pumping like mad. But as soon as she got to the street, she wished she hadn't pumped quite so hard, because she'd forgotten that Amber lived at the *top* of the hill.

"I'm gonna die," she said to herself as she flew down the street. She slammed on the brakes and came to an abrupt stop.

"Get a grip," she told herself, then she began scootering

again, this time, just coasting down the hill.

When she got to the bottom of the street, she began to push off with her foot again.

"Are you a princess?" a little boy of about four standing outside with his mom asked her as she passed by his house.

"Ha! Far from it," she said, making a mental note to never ever wear a dress again that made her look like some sicky-sweet princess character.

She was starting to get hot with all the scootering, and sweat was sliding down her forehead. The hem of her dress was dragging on the sidewalk, and she could feel her hair whip around her face like she was in a wind tunnel.

The final block leading to the school was uphill and Zibby huffed her hardest to get up it in record time.

"Faster," she told herself, "faster. I've got to get there."

As she turned the final corner leading to the school, she saw a sight that made her heart sing: the limo, just pulling up into the school driveway.

She'd made it! She'd made it on time!

She ditched the scooter in the bushes and ran to meet the limo, breathless.

"What happened to you?" asked Gertrude as she and Sarah exited.

"Yeah, we tried to get the driver to wait, but Amber insisted he get going so we wouldn't be late," said Sarah.

"I forgot my bag, so I had to run back in," Zibby explained. "Then I missed the limo. But the good thing is, I'm here now! Let's get to the bathroom and change – quick!"

The three girls started out toward the bathroom.

"So, how was the limo ride?" Zibby asked.

"Not great," said Sarah. "They had this ginormous TV screen turned to a boring football game – the boys wanted to watch. And they had these really gross spicy peanuts for a snack."

"Yeah, and the driver wouldn't let us open the sunroof even though it was really hot and none of the windows rolled down," added Gertrude.

"I guess I didn't miss much then," said Zibby, feeling happy she'd scootered rather than limoed.

When the girls got to the bathroom, Zibby dropped her bag and immediately began tugging on the zipper of Big Pink. But, just like she couldn't zip up the dress on her own, she needed help to unzip it.

"Can you unzip this for me please?" Zibby asked Sarah, turning around so her back faced Sarah.

"Sure," said Sarah as she grabbed onto the zipper and gave it a big yank.

"Oops, I think it might be stuck," she said.

"What?" asked Zibby anxiously.

"Wait a minute." Sarah pulled on the zipper again, but it still didn't budge.

"Can't you get it down?" asked Zibby, her voice rising.

"Well, not yet," admitted Sarah.

"Oh my gosh! Help! I'm a prisoner of Big Pink!" Zibby screamed.

"I think what's happening is that the material of the dress is caught in the zipper," said Sarah. "I need something to push the material away. Nail scissors would work. Anyone have any?"

"No," Zibby and Gertrude said in unison.

"Hmm." Sarah frowned. "Maybe a safety pin?"

"I don't have that either," said Zibby.

"Me neither," Gertrude shook her head.

"Help!" Zibby said again, trying to pull the dress over her head, but it wouldn't fit over her shoulders. Just then, she felt something prick her thigh. She immediately knew what it was. Amber's fish fork – poking her through her skirt and tights. And then she got one of her Very Good Ideas. Maybe this stupid fork might actually be good for something!

She reached up under her dress and pulled the fork out of her jean skirt pocket.

"Try this," she said as she handed the fork to Sarah.

"You still have this?" Sarah asked, looking surprised.

"Yeah, I keep forgetting to give it back to Amber," said Zibby.

"Let's hope it works," said Sarah.

Sarah fiddled with the zipper for a minute or two with the fork, when finally the zipper unstuck. "I got it!" she said triumphantly and pulled the zipper down.

"Thank you!" said Zibby, stepping out of Big Pink.

Sarah gave Zibby the fork, and Zibby placed it back in her skirt pocket. Then she quickly put on her tutu, feather boa, and hat.

"I'm ready!" she announced.

"Me, too," said Gertrude. She looked Totally Crazy in a bright purple vintage dress, a yellow tutu, a red-and-white-striped scarf, beret, and red knee-high rain boots.

"I'm not – at all," said Sarah. She had been so preoccupied with Zibby's Great Zipper Crisis she hadn't had a chance to change. "Why don't you two go without me? I'll catch up."

Zibby hated to leave without Sarah, but she was eager to get the revolt started. She was worried if they were any later, there wouldn't be anyone to see their non-red carpet entrance.

"Are you sure?" Zibby asked.

"Yes. It's okay. Just go!" she shouted as she pushed Zibby and Gertrude out the bathroom door.

The two girls dashed out of the bathroom and down the hallway that lead to the cafeteria. When they turned the final corner, they saw the red carpet, set off by guard rails. Amber, Camille and Savannah were just starting to walk down it, giving the movie star wave and walk, and the rest of the sixth graders were lined up behind them. A photographer, as Amber had promised, was standing on the sidelines snapping pictures.

But instead of joining the rest of the kids, Zibby and Gertrude made a detour to the bushes next to the cafeteria door and picked up a soccer ball Zibby had hidden there. Then they walked to the top of the red carpet but instead of stepping on it, side-stepped it completely. Zibby set the ball down on the ground, and the two girls walked parallel to the carpet, kicking the ball back and forth the entire way.

When they got to the cafeteria door, Zibby booted the ball back into the bushes, and then she and Gertrude gave each other a Mickey Mouse wave. Then they looked back at the photographer, who was hovering near them, and they smiled and crossed their eyes at the camera.

"That was awesome," said Zibby. "I'm just sorry Sarah didn't make it. Where the heck is she?"

She looked around for Sarah one more time, but instead a group of kids came off the Red Carpet, and Zibby and

Gertrude were swept into the cafeteria. And the first person Zibby ran into inside was Amber!

"Zibby, what are you and Gertrude doing, wearing those clothes and doing that stupid wave and kicking a soccer ball?" she asked snottily.

"We're just making the sixth-grade dance fun – like it should be," retorted Zibby. "We thought about it and we didn't feel comfortable walking down a red carpet or wearing dresses."

"But you were wearing them at my house," said Amber.

"We changed when we got here," explained Zibby. "We know it's a fancy ball and everything, but we just don't feel like we can follow all the red carpet rules."

Amber looked at her as if Zibby had lost her mind. "Whatever, Zibby," she spat out. "Like I care what you do anyway."

But then Amber looked at Zibby's outfit, from head to toe, and then smiled. "I will say one thing for you, though, Zibby," she added. "When you do something, you do it in a big way."

"Yes, I do," said Zibby. She scanned the room, taking in the chocolate fountain placed in the center of the room, the tables of sandwiches and tea, the fancy flower decorations scattered around, and the dance floor with posters of dancing couples hanging from the ceiling. "And you know what? So do you, Amber."

"Thank you very much," Amber said as she gave a little curtsy.

And just then, Zibby realized she'd forgotten to thank Amber's parents for the ball, like she'd promised her mom she would, so she figured she'd thank Amber instead. Because one thing was true. This ball idea was totally dopey, but Amber and her parents had gone all out – and then some – trying to make it nice.

"Hey, thanks for doing all this for the class," said Zibby. "I'm not that into this type of thing, but I know you've worked hard, and so have your parents."

"Wait – you're thanking me?" asked Amber, looking somewhat shocked.

"Uh ... yes, that's what it sounds like," said Zibby.

"You know what? You're the first person to thank me. In the entire class," said Amber. "So Zibby Payne, even though you are being a pain right now with this weird outfit thing you have going on and that soccer ball entrance, I want to thank *you* for saying that."

"You're welcome," said Zibby. Wow! Amber hadn't thanked her for anything all year long!

And for an instant, she was feeling so warm and fuzzy toward Amber that she started to tell her about the rest of the Red Carpet Revolt activities she had planned in order to give her a heads-up. But just as she was about to, a gang of girls, including Gertrude, Lyla, Katherine, Grace, and Franny ran up to Zibby and separated her from Amber.

"Gertrude told us all about the anti-ball, and we think it's great," Katherine said as she grabbed Zibby by the arm in excitement.

"You look so cute," Lyla complimented her. "And comfy." She looked down at Zibby's high-tops. "My feet feel like someone is squeezing all the blood out of my toes."

Lyla's feet were jammed into black pointy pumps.

"Your feet are going to be shaped like triangles by the end of the evening," joked Zibby.

"I know," nodded Lyla.

"And my gloves are totally bugging me," sighed Grace, who was wearing white gloves up to her elbows. "I can't believe I even wore them."

"So take them off," suggested Gertrude.

"Okay, I will," declared Grace, ripping off her gloves.

"And I'll take off these toe-crunching shoes," said Lyla as she kicked off her pumps. "That feels much better. I just wish I had something crazy to wear."

"Take my boa," offered Zibby. She pulled it off and handed it to Lyla.

"Thanks, Zibby, I will," said Lyla happily, wrapping the feather boa around her neck.

"Looking good," Zibby said. She hadn't planned on other girls coming over to their revolt, but if they wanted to, that was fine with her. She was happy to be spreading anti-ball cheer with Gertrude.

But just then, she saw something that took away her anti-ball cheer. It was Sarah, standing over by the dance floor. She was *still* wearing her dress!

CHAPTER 14

FOOD FOR THOUGHT

"You didn't change!" Zibby ran over to Sarah after saying a quick "Excuse me for a second" to the other girls.

"No, I didn't," Sarah looked down at the floor.

"What happened? Did you get stuck in your dress too?" asked Zibby.

"No." Sarah still didn't look up.

"What then? Why are you still in it?" Zibby asked.

Sarah finally met Zibby's eyes. "I'm sorry, Zibby. I really meant to change, but I just couldn't. I like this dress. I love this dress, actually. So I kept it on."

"Oh," said Zibby as she slowly but surely realized that Sarah didn't change on purpose. "But I thought you wanted to dress crazy with us."

"I thought I did. And I really planned on it. But at the last minute, I just couldn't make myself. I hope you're not too mad at me," added Sarah.

"Oh, well, I'm not," said Zibby. Actually, she was disappointed Sarah wasn't going along with that part of the revolt, but she didn't want to make Sarah feel any guiltier than she already felt. Besides, if you thought about it, she should have known that Sarah would want to wear her dress. After all, Sarah told her how much she liked it. "It's okay," she added.

"That's good," said Sarah, looking relieved.

"Oh, but you missed the un-red carpet walk too!" exclaimed Zibby. "It was so much fun kicking the soccer ball!"

"I'm sorry I missed it. I just went down the red carpet since I didn't want to walk alone," said Sarah.

"You walked down it?" Zibby was surprised. Even if she'd had to walk alone, there's no way she would have done that.

"Yeah, everyone else was, so I just sort of followed," Sarah shrugged apologetically.

And just then, Zibby had a Big Revelation. Because she started thinking back about how it was Sarah's whole idea to go undercover and take more of Amber's classes and go to her pre-party. Was it possible that she only did all that so she herself could learn more about manners? Sarah had liked some of the classes, and she certainly seemed to enjoy her manicure-pedicure at Amber's house.

"Hey, was the real reason you had us go undercover so you could be a part of the Manner's Ball after all?" Zibby asked.

"No," said Sarah firmly. "No way. I just thought it would make a better Revolt."

"Really?" pressed Zibby.

"Really," said Sarah. But she didn't sound very convincing to Zibby. And maybe that was a discussion for another time, or maybe Sarah really hadn't even known herself that she wanted to be part of Amber's lessons. But whatever the truth was, Zibby let it drop. There were more important things to do ... like keeping this Red Carpet Revolt moving ... and ... also, snagging one of those really juicy-looking strawberries over by the fountain and dip it in some flowing chocolate.

"Okay then. Want to hit the fountain?" she asked Sarah.

"You know it," said Sarah, smiling.

The two girls walked over to the fountain, where a crowd of kids were dipping the fruit and cookie wafers into the streams of chocolate.

"Yummy," said Zibby, dipping in a strawberry and tasting it. She was about to dip the strawberry in for another dose of chocolate, when a sign, posted on the side of the fountain and written in fancy cursive script, caught her eye: "It's not polite to double dip"

"Woops," she said, stopping mid-dip, and she ate the rest of the strawberry au natural.

Then she remembered something. "Wait! I have a contribution to the desserts," she cried out. She reached into her bag and pulled out the gummy worms, and then dumped them in a big pile alongside the chocolate fountain. They didn't look very appetizing next to the fruit and cookie pile-up, but still, maybe someone would want them.

"So there you two are," Gertrude came running up to them. "I've been filling everyone in on the anti-ball. They all love the idea! Hey," she suddenly noticed Sarah's clothes. "You're still in your dress," she said.

"Yeah – long story," said Sarah.

"Okay, well, tell me some other time then," Gertrude grabbed a strawberry. "Oh, I've got to try this," she dipped it in chocolate. "Rad," she smiled. "Oh, and on the topic of food, has anyone checked out the finger sandwiches?"

"No." Zibby made a face.

"Come on, let's go look," said Gertrude walking toward the sandwich table, where Amber and Camille were standing. Zibby and Sarah followed her.

"This isn't what they showed us at the caterer's," Amber was whining as she pulled apart one of the sandwiches to reveal a yellow creamy filling and, just as Zibby had predicted, green stuff that looked like grass. "This looks pukey," shuddered Amber.

Zibby and Sarah didn't want to try one, but Gertrude did, and she confirmed Amber's opinion. "Yuck," she whispered to Zibby.

"I heard that," Amber shot her the evil eye.

"Sorry," Gertrude shrugged apologetically. "But you even said they didn't look good."

Zibby was actually feeling a little sorry for Amber – and for the rest of the kids stuck with the grass sandwiches – when she glanced over at the cafeteria door and saw a Pizza Palace deliveryman standing there holding four large pizzas!

"Pizza's here," she said excitedly to Gertrude and Sarah.

"What?" Amber asked suspiciously, frowning, as she too, noticed the delivery man.

"Hey, it's the answer to your problem," said Zibby. "Pizza! We ordered a bunch of Everythings, and here they are right now."

"You ordered pizzas ... for my fancy ball?" Amber sputtered.

"Yep," said Zibby. "It just wouldn't be a sixth-grade dance without pizza."

"Zibby, are you trying to do your own thing again?" Amber asked.

"Um, yes. Again, we're just trying to have fun. And, we'll share!"

"Hmm," Amber said as she narrowed her eyes. "Well, I am pretty hungry, and these sandwiches are pretty gross, so, it's okay with me, I guess."

"Great," said Zibby cheerfully, even though of course, she wouldn't have done anything differently if Amber hadn't approved. "I'll go get the pizzas right now."

But just as she was headed toward the deliveryman to take the pizzas, Miss Cannon approached him. And she turned him around and started to walk him *out* the door!

CHAPTER 15

AND EVERYONE HAD A BALL

"Wait a minute," Zibby pleaded, now running with Amber in tow. "Please, Miss Cannon, wait. That's our pizza. I ordered it and I have the money to pay for it."

"We already have food. And Zibby, what are you and Gertrude wearing tonight, anyway?" asked Miss Cannon, giving Zibby a stern look. She herself was dressed in a practical-looking knee-length black cocktail dress.

"Fun, comfy clothes." Zibby glossed over their outfits in case Miss Cannon would get mad at that too. "Now, please, let me pay for the pizza."

"Pizza is not on the menu tonight," she said firmly.

"It's okay with me, Miss Cannon, if that means anything," said Amber, giving a big dimply smile.

"Really? But your parents already provided sandwiches. Won't they be offended?"

"Don't worry, I'm sure the extra munchies are fine with them," said Amber.

Miss Cannon pulled on her pinky and looked a little cross. "I don't understand you at all. You wanted a fancy ball, but now you want pizza. Can't you girls make up your minds?" she asked.

"We have, Miss Cannon, and we think pizza would be a welcome addition to the sixth-grade dance," said Zibby. She looked hopefully at her teacher.

"Oh, keep it, then, I guess," said Miss Cannon, walking off. "Sixth graders," she muttered under her breath, shaking her head.

Zibby showed the delivery man where to put the pizza – on the table next to the sandwiches – and paid him. Before leaving, he also set down two big bottles of soda and some plastic cups.

And the next thing Zibby knew, she was the most popular girl at the ball.

A hoard of sixth graders surrounded her and started grabbing pieces of pizza and swigging soda.

"Good work, tomboy," said Matthew, moving in for the food. He was holding a half-eaten finger sandwich, and he quickly chucked into the nearest trash can. "And cool outfit, too."

"Thanks," smiled Zibby as the compliments on the anti-ball fare continued to roll in.

"The Everything is ... everything good!" raved Franny.

"Love those chocolate chips," Gertrude chimed in, reaching for a second slice.

"And this soda is a lot better than tea!" said Lyla. "I was scared to even touch that fancy china in case I broke it."

Pretty soon, most everyone was gathered around the pizza, laughing and joking, except for pizza-phobic Bernice who was talking to Miss Cannon, and for Amber, Camille, and Savannah, who were out on the dance floor.

Camille and Savannah had gotten the idea to try to waltz, and Amber was also on the dance floor, acting as their coach.

"One, two, three, one, two, three," she was trying to get

them to stay in rhythm. But the truth was, neither girl seemed to be a much better waltzer than Zibby. Camille kept stepping on Savannah's feet, giving Zibby nasty flashbacks of her Aunt Bev dancing experience.

"Why don't you guys come have some pizza instead?" Zibby walked over to ask them. After all, Amber was the reason Miss Cannon let them have the pizza anyway.

"In a sec, thanks," said Amber, before coming over to her, looking Totally Discouraged. "Camille and Savannah can't waltz, and something tells me nobody else is going to want to, don't you think?" she asked.

"I think you're right," Zibby said.

"I guess our class isn't like the kids on *Rich, Blonde & Bored*," Amber sighed, looking at the now-deserted finger sandwich and tea table and then at all the Happy Pizza Eaters.

"Maybe not," nodded Zibby politely, while inside she was screaming, "Ya think?" "But you know," she smiled. "I have a solution to the waltzing problem too."

"Really?" Amber looked interested.

"Yeah, I have my iPod and Anthony's speakers, and I was planning on playing more modern songs."

"So what's on your play list?" asked Amber.

"A lot of classic rock, like the Beatles – my favorite, of course – but there's also a group you'll like – BB5." That was one of the "unZibby" groups she'd put on the playlist at the very last minute, just in case.

"Really?" Amber perked up. "That might be okay with *moi* and my peeps!"

"Give me a sec, then," said Zibby. "Oh, and do you mind turning off that waltzing music?"

Amber hurried off to turn down the ballroom dancing music. Zibby reached into her bag and pulled out the iPod and speakers and set them up next to the dance floor.

She selected the song she was looking for from the playlist, and BB5's newest hit single, "Don't Ever Forget Me, Babe, Even though I've Already Forgotten You," came on.

"Cool song," yelled out Grace. On the dance floor, Camille and Savannah broke apart from their waltzing stance and began jumping around as if they were BB5 back-up dancers.

"'I've forgotten you, oh yeah,'" Camille yelled, flipping off a high-heeled wedge. Within seconds, she'd kicked off the other one. Soon other kids, barefoot, also joined her and Savannah.

"Well, we did it," Zibby beamed triumphantly to Sarah and Gertrude, who'd come over to join her. "We actually made the sixth-grade dance fun – and not just for us, but everyone!"

The three girls hugged each other.

"Ouch," cried out Sarah. "Something poked me."

"Oh no," Zibby felt in her jean skirt pocket. The fish fork. She *still* hadn't returned it to Amber.

"Be right back," Zibby said to her friends. Then she walked over to Amber, who was standing on the edge of the dance floor.

"This is yours," she said. "I had it fixed awhile ago, but I keep forgetting to give it to you."

"Oh, thanks," said Amber, taking the fork. "I figured this puppy was long gone – that you lost it out on the soccer field or something."

"Sorry it took me so long to give it back," said Zibby.

"Oh hey, I think I'll get some pizza now," said Amber.

"But just don't expect me to eat it with this fish fork."

"Using your mom's antique fish fork on pizza? No way," Zibby shook her head and smiled, amazed that she and Amber were now finally agreeing on so many things. "Now *that* really would be bad manners!"

THE END

About the author:

The **"Zibby Payne"** series was created by self-professed Total Tomboy **Alison Bell** who lives just outside of Los Angeles in South Pasadena, California. She has written several books for tweens and teens, including *Let's Party!* and *Fearless Fashion* from the **"What's Your Style?"** series (Lobster Press), and her articles have appeared in *Sassy*, *YM*, and *TEEN*. Visit Alison at www.alisonbellauthor.com.